River Blues

(A Jason Colefield Mystery)

By

Doc Macomber

Floating Word Press, LLC
Portland, Oregon

Floating Word Press, LLC
1017 SW Morrison St. Suite 215
Portland, Oregon 97205

www.floatingwordpress.com

Library of Congress Control Number: 2020905653

Soft Cover ISBN: 978-1-941297-10-0

COVER DESIGNED BY DIVERSITY DESIGN STUDIOS
Editor: Martha Cowen
Author photograph Copyright © 2014 by Ty Hitzemann
Cover painting inspired by Ben Will. Modified by
Mary Jane Haake, Copyright © 2020
by Doc Haake Productions

Manufactured in the United States of America

Printing Number

987654321

First Edition

For my good bud, Eddy...

1

There's a time in life when you realize that the glory days are gone, the drive that once was has dribbled away, leaving behind only a hail of alcoholism and years of regret. It can be stunting. It can be dangerous and depressing.

Multnomah County River Patrol Deputy Jason Colefield wasn't sure why he was feeling so melancholy that Friday morning in August. He was fighting it, attempting to be mindful instead, and enjoy the morning cruise on the Columbia with his new partner.

"I hated what I had to do, but the devil drives us."

Those were the haunting words from Ken Bruen's book, *Ammunition.* He'd been reading Bruen earlier on the john, which was an appropriate place to read crime fiction. Bruen always captivated him with characters he couldn't shake. Then, all that changed when the 911 call from dispatch had come in. Maybe it was all just words, or maybe more — like an early warning of what awaited.

At the helm, he grew restless staring at the Columbia River, an endless mirror of blue gray water that he'd seen a thousand times. He wanted to believe it was beautiful, the best a man could ask for, this silent connection with nature, an opportunity to lose oneself. He had before. Time and again. A Canadian goose flying by could swallow him up in its grace; the magnificent way its dark wings would spread and rhythmically stroke the sky like a lover's wanton legs. And then a moment later, he'd hear phantom gunshots, be yanked from the dream. The sky would spill blood. He'd be back to a dark past — futile, lifeless, no longer able to focus on the glistening rippled river that had calmed him moments before.

He finally glanced over at Deputy Beverly "Bev" Manning as the boat veered south, over the choppy confluence of where the Willamette dumped into the Columbia. He'd heard Manning had just gotten out of a bad marriage and was off men, which suited him fine.

The moment she walked inside headquarters; she had sized him up. Any good cop would. The lieutenant seemed happy to have her aboard. So did the rest of the crew. Yet, he wasn't so sure.

Her eyes radiated an intensity that he could feel 6-feet away. Maybe she'd be a partner who would carry her own weight. Only time would tell. Yet, it felt very odd to be working with a woman after so many years.

Less than a half-hour after the call had come in, they were approaching downtown. Manning spotted the shiny sparkling glass stacks, of the Waterfront Pearl Condominiums, a short distance ahead. He backed off the throttle, gliding the aluminum boat toward the west side of the riverbank.

On land, a few blue uniforms were mingling about trying to keep pedestrians and bicyclists away from the scene. A KGW news crew was on site filming. Colefield didn't see Feinstein anywhere. He glanced up by the fountain that separated the two towers and extended along the rear of the complex before spotting a short man who looked like the detective, standing in a rumpled suit, jotting something down on a notepad. The man must have heard the river patrol boat and turned to look. The ruddy face was not Feinstein but could have passed as his twin. Colefield figured he was a Fed.

He killed the engine. The momentary silence amplified the slightest sounds. The riverbank scraped against the metal hull as they drifted ashore.

Deputy Manning jumped out first looking for a sturdy tie-off, looping the bow line around a jagged piece of concrete, after which, they hiked up the embankment toward the excitement.

A paved bike path linked Waterfront Park to the south. To the north, the path dead-ended shortly after the towers at the former stables of the Mounted Patrol next door to the Old Centennial Mills site.

Colefield remembered all of it. The Waterfront Pearl was one of the last condo projects of its kind before the luxury apartment splurge ignited. Old Town, the Pearl District, and the West End, were all under major development. Old buildings were being torn down. The industrial appeal as he knew as a child was being destroyed. In its place towers of glass and steel that had limited architecture appeal, were shooting up like weeds. The city he knew as a kid was nearly extinct.

Several cops stood around on the manicured grass in front of the fountain with their notebooks in hand, looking bored. A police photographer was on site running around with a Nikon snapping photographs. The paramedics stood back watching from the sidelines and a few plain-clothed detectives were milling about, talking with a few of the residents. The area had been taped off. Several tenants were out on their decks watching the activity from above. Everyone seemed to be waiting for either the Medical Examiner or Brass to arrive. He finally spotted Feinstein. Standing knee-deep in water in the middle of the fountain in hip-waders, his sleeves rolled up past the elbow, drawn to something in the water. And then Colefield saw the woman's body, silhouetted in shadow. The barefoot brunette floated face-down in the trickling water. Her paisley kimono soaked in blood.

The deputies moved in closer, to a patch of grass at the fountain's edge. A sign nearby read: *"Please keep pets out of the fountain."*

Colefield caught Feinstein's attention and waved. Officer Manning took it all in.

"Why is it always a woman?" She said.

Colefield didn't figure the comment needed a response. He was so accustomed to finding bodies in the river that he felt some relief in this setting. This one hadn't been floating around for weeks. Decay — the ripe stench of a bloating, off-gassing of a fermented corpse — hadn't set it.

Feinstein splashed over to the deputies in his bulky waders. His pencil-thin tie thrown over his shoulder.

"Hey, Bev."

"Hey, Feinstein."

"How's this rogue treating you?"

"I've got no complaints so far. Got an ID on the dead girl?"

"We're asking around. There's a guy on the eight-floor, thinks she lives in the North Tower."

"Who found her?"

"A resident on the sixth-floor. They were having coffee on their balcony when they saw her in the fountain."

Colefield asked: "What's her age?"

"I'd put her around 30. Her face took a good hit on the concrete. No jewelry or tattoos. Once the ME takes a closer examination, will have a better idea. Would one of you give me a hand?" Feinstein put his arm out and Colefield pulled him out of the fountain onto dry ground.

"Is she wearing anything under the kimono?"

"No..."

"Any signs of sexual assault?"

"Too early to tell."

"Are you thinking homicide or suicide?"

"Once I get into her condo maybe I can answer that. We're waiting on the ME before we make a move."

Colefield looked up at the twin towers and counted the number of floors. There were ten. Most had balconies hanging out over the fountain. She could have fallen anywhere. But by the amount of blood that was present, Colefield presumed it was one of the upper floors.

If you had a unit facing east the towers had a good view of the Willamette River, Mt Hood, the Broadway and Freemont Bridges. They sat directly across the river from a turn-of-the-century grain elevator where a cargo ship was docked.

The detective sat down on the edge of the water feature and began removing his hip waders. "See that boat across the river?" Feinstein pointed toward the ship moored at the old grain silo. "I'd like you two to go interview the captain and crew. See what you can learn..."

"A body in a fountain is stretching our jurisdiction, don't you think?"

"Colefield don't bust my balls. You patrol this river. You know the slang those guys talk — all that nautical jargon. I could use your cooperation."

"If you want to get technical," Manning added, "she is in the water."

Colefield ignored the comment. He focused instead on the ship. It was named the *Piranha,* flying a Panamanian flag — red, white, and blue with two opposing stars. Overall, the length looked to be about 100 meters, the same size as a football field. Her decks were red, her hull black. Four cranes for loading cargo stood idle. She had a tall pilot house. Plenty of opportunity for someone to view across the river.

"I suppose we could make a case with the Lieutenant."

"Anyone working the bridge would have a bird's-eye view of this place. See what you can find out. How's your Spanish, Manning?"

"Does *uno cerveza por favor* count?"

Feinstein cracked a smile. "According to one of the residents here, the ship arrived last night around 10 pm.

My guess, the girl took her plunge between midnight and 2 AM."

He set the hip waders aside and put his leather shoes on.

Colefield turned to speak to Feinstein when an earnest woman in a white lab coat, lugging a medical bag, called out the detective's name.

Feinstein spun round. "Let me know what you find out."

2

The deputies avoided the reporters and returned to their patrol boat. Manning kicked some mud from her boot and then climbed aboard taking the helm.

He tossed in the bow line and shoved off. From where he sat he could see Feinstein and the ME pointing up at one of the balconies. Colefield eventually looked at Manning, aware he knew nothing about her. "So how good is your Spanish?"

"My first ex was Hispanic. I picked up a few things..."

"Like what?"

"Like fuck you ... and the horse you rode in on."

Colefield cracked a smile.

"See if you can make radio contact with the helm. Let them know we're coming aboard."

Manning picked up the microphone and made the call. She spoke a few lines in Spanish and then switched to English. She kept it short and simple.

"Done."

"Who'd you speak with?"

"Second in charge. A Lieutenant Luis."

"Where's the captain?"

"He doesn't know."

The patrol boat idled aft of the enormous ship and fell into shadow. Colefield told Manning to keep some distance until they checked the docks. They only had a limited view, but everything ashore looked quiet.

In some sick way, the fact that it was so deserted disappointed Colefield. He needed to shake his funk. He figured a good ass-kicking would do it. Not the smartest way to relieve stress, which is what his VA counselor would say. Maybe it was time for a visit, before someone got seriously hurt.

Manning circled around and looked where they could tie off. The dock was built tall to accommodate bulk container vessels, not small watercraft.

"What now?" Manning asked, staring up at the tall ship.

"Call Luis back and see where they want us."

After placing the radio call, Manning motored in close to amidship. A few minutes later, one of the crew leaned over the starboard deck, waved down to them, and tossed a rope ladder over the side.

Colefield tied a line to it, so their boat wouldn't float off. Manning went first. She stepped onto the gunnel, got a foothold on the rope, and began climbing.

Colefield watched her effortlessly pull herself topside. It was his turn now and he felt a little out of practice, a little out of shape, compared to his partner, and when he reached the top, he was out of breath. He gazed down into the empty cargo holds, feeling a little dizzy. Manning walked over and stood beside him.

"You OK?"

"Don't gloat..."

"Feinstein was right about you."

"What do you mean?"

"You're charming demeanor."

About then, a warning bell sounded ashore at the silo. Men in hardhats appeared and climbed up old ladders to the conveyor control tower. Colefield knew what was coming next when the loud rumbling began.

"Let's get out of here!"

Within moments, grain flooded into the cargo holds, shooting a geyser of fine dust skyward. Dozens of excited seagulls began squawking and feeding off the grain trails blowing in all directions.

Manning covered her mouth and nose and looked for shelter from the swirling grit.

Colefield managed to grab her wrist and pull her out of the tunnel sucking them in. Someone from the pilot house was shouting for them to hurry.

Momentarily the dust cleared enough for them to spot a young officer in a white uniform waving from the bridge.

"Take the rearward stairs!" he instructed.

They found the door at the stern and began climbing stairs. The young lieutenant greeted them in the pilot house and hustled them inside, securing a steel door behind them.

"I am Luis Canelé, second in command," he said. "I very much apologize for the dust, but we are under a very tight deadline. And we are worried the Longshoremen will strike."

Luis's ethnic features gave him a vibrant appearance. He shook their hands.

Colefield figured Luis was just doing his job and let it go, focusing instead on the bridge — the familiar navigational equipment, radios, and backup systems, he'd known so well. He'd been aboard plenty of ships like this. For now, his interest was the view out the windows. Feinstein, as usual, had predicted correctly. Anyone on duty that night would have a decent, unobstructed view across the river of the twin towers.

Manning picked bits of grain from the corner of her eyes.

"Can I bring you some water," Luis asked. "If you prefer coffee, we have plenty."

Manning shook her head. Colefield concurred, swiping dust from his nose.

Luis picked up his coffee mug. "Then what can I do for you, officers?"

"We won't take up much of your time, Lieutenant Luis," Colefield said. "I'll get right to the point. We're investigating an incident that occurred across the river last night. We're hoping someone aboard may have witnessed it."

"Yes, go on…"

"A woman jumped off her balcony. Or she may have been pushed. We don't know for sure which." He pointed out to Luis where it occurred.

"When exactly did this happened?"

"Between 10pm and 2 am. I understand your ship was in port?"

"I suppose it is possible that one of my crew could have seen something. But no one has come forward."

"Do we have your permission to talk with them?"

The Lieutenant nodded. "Of course, we shall take the walk together. First, I must get someone to watch the bridge. One *momento*, please."

The Lieutenant picked up the ship's microphone and spoke Spanish. After he was finished, he turned his charming eyes toward Manning. "Someone will be along shortly."

"Who was on watch last night?" Colefield asked.

Luis responded slowly. "I was, sir."

"And did you happen to see a young woman on the balcony?"

Luis checked his watch. "No — I did not."

"Where was the captain?"

"He took shore-leave after we docked. I would say that he left the ship around 2300 hours."

"Where did he go?"

"You will need to ask him when he returns."

Colefield looked at Manning, who was checking everything out. "How many crew are aboard?"

"Thirteen including the captain and I."

"Do they all speak English?"

"It is fifty-fifty for those who speak. Although we fly the colors of Panama, not all our crew is Panamanian. The captain is — three others and I as well. The rest are mixed.

They come from Honduras, Costa Rica and Nicaragua. Our boatswain is from the Philippines."

The door to the bridge opened. In walked another officer wearing a uniform. His hair was pomaded back, his skin darker than the Lieutenant's and he was a head shorter. He approached the Lieutenant and then stopped and waited further instructions.

Luis spoke to him in Spanish. Manning indicated to Colefield that she couldn't understand everything.

"Unfortunately, he is of no help to you officers. He saw nothing last night either."

"When do you expect your captain to return?" Manning asked.

"We hope soon," Luis replied.

They used a rear hatch and wound their way down steep stairs to mid-ship. The smell of fresh paint reminded Colefield of his Navy days, when he was assigned to one of the Maritime Interception Operation (MIO) teams. He'd boarded ships like this bulk freighter many times to inspect for contraband. It was part of their mission when he was assigned to the Central Command Fleet. Most of the memories were pleasant. But there were always unknowns that no amount of training could prepare you for ... and for this reason he still had fragments that flicked through his mind.

Lieutenant led them down a second flight of stairs and then stopped in front of another steel door. He spun the locking-wheel and then pushed it open and motioned for Manning to go first.

Next, they passed by a storage bunker and then entered a galley. The area was unoccupied. Several tables and benches were set up. Two large coffee pots steamed on a table in the corner. The room smelled like bacon grease. Next was the crew's quarters. Dark with only a dim, yellowish light lit, bunks on either side. The smell of crusty socks and B.O in the air. It had been modified to accommodate a larger crew. Colefield remembered spending plenty of time in a similar coffin-sized bunk, legs wedged in the small compartments, so cramped up they throbbed at night. He felt a familiar phantom pain in his right knee.

Blackout curtains had been installed, like most cargo ships. These were pulled back on several of the bunks where snoring could be heard.

One of the crew was glued to a Spanish Swim Suit Edition of Sports Illustrated when the Lieutenant forcefully clapped his hands and brought them to attention.

Even the weary ones snapped to and hopped down from their top bunks. They all looked foreign. No white skin in the bunch, five in all, Colefield noted. That still left five unaccounted for. The lieutenant spoke to them in Spanish and they answered his questions. He then turned and looked at the deputies, shaking his head.

"They know nothing," he said.

Colefield studied their faces. "Does your crew work in shifts?"

"Yes."

Manning followed behind. "Were all the crew accounted for last night?"

The Lieutenant replied casually. "Yes."

Getting down into the engine room required a descent of more steep stairs. The Lieutenant led the way, not saying a word.

Rearward, a narrow catwalk constructed from metal grating ran along both sides of the large-bore MAN engine.

"That's one huge "F-ing engine," Manning blurted out.

The area smelled of diesel and was stiflingly hot. A deep rumbling echoed through the walls. Colefield figured it was vibrations from the grain elevators, dumping into the holds.

He stepped down on the platform and kept an eye on Manning. He was hot. Sweat dripped down his forehead. He imagined Manning was hotter with her head of hair tucked up under her cap. She lifted her hat and swiped perspiration from her forehead. It was a good fifteen degrees hotter here than anywhere else on the ship.

Up ahead, two shirtless mechanics covered in grease were swearing at a stubborn fuel canister. They were trying to get at the clogged filter inside. Colefield remembered all the cursing that went on aboard his ship. That's not to say, there wasn't whistling and singing. Whenever the crew had been granted shore leave; they sang like songbirds. He figured these guys were no different.

On the opposite side, two of the crew worked on a hydraulic pump. They had disassembled a portion of it and were inspecting parts. One of the mechanics noticed them and signaled to his buddy, who got the other crew member's attention by setting off a chain-reaction of whistling. They all gathered single file before the Lieutenant.

The Lieutenant smiled proudly over at Manning. "A tight ship, yes?"

He spoke to the men in Spanish and then turned toward Colefield. "Nothing either, I'm afraid."

Manning concurred that the Lieutenant was telling them the truth.

There is still one other," Luis said. "Come. Follow me and please be careful. The grating may be slippery."

Colefield took one last look at the men. If they were withholding information, it didn't show in their weary eyes.

Once they reached the deck, it took a few moments for their eyes to adjust to the bright sunlight. Colefield patted his vest pockets and found his sunglasses and quickly put them on. Dust was still swirling about, churning up out of ship's holds, but the equipment had stopped running. They made it to a clearing on the aft deck. Up ahead, seagulls were cawing and circling the sky.

Nearby, an old Panamanian man was laughing. Donning a dirty apron cinched around his rotund waist, welding a gravy-stained roasting pan, he playfully tossed scraps to the birds.

"There stands the most important man aboard," the Lieutenant said proudly, shielding his eyes from bits of debris. He called out to the cook. "Felipe! Come here, please!"

The man clearly understood English. He set the roasting pan down, secured the lid and waddled toward them. He was a clumsy looking man with friendly eyes and nearly as wide as he was tall. His thinning hair was gray.

"Felipe — these officers would like to know if you saw anything last night over at those twin towers across the river. A woman fell from one of the balconies. They are looking for witnesses."

Felipe swallowed hard. His smile vanished. He now seemed apprehensive to look where the Lieutenant was pointing. Colefield noticed a fresh burn on his right hand.

"Felipe, did you see anything last night?"

Felipe refused to make eye contact.

The Lieutenant crossed his arms, waiting. "She is dead. They are trying to get to the bottom of it."

Felipe covered his mouth and suddenly bent over as if he was about to vomit.

"We are waiting!"

Felipe stood up slowly, sweating profusely now. He covered his face with his hands and sobbed. "It was all so terrible."

The Lieutenant looked shocked by the outburst. "The officers need to know what you saw."

"Terrible, terrible, terrible…"

The Lieutenant softened, stepped forward and rested his hand on the man's shoulder, attempting to calm him down.

The man stifled back his tears. He swiped a sleeve over his soaked face, sniffled and wagged his head back and forth in denial. Dust collected on his damp skin.

The man looked down at the ground. "I did not want to believe it."

"Tell us everything, Felipe. The officers need to provide information to their superiors."

The man sucked in his gut, trying to pull himself together. "I was smoking, sir, taking a break from my galley duties. I look across the river and there she was, on her balcony, a lovely white dove. All alone at first, staring up at the stars. I watched her for a long while until my cigarette went out. Then somebody else appeared. That's when it happened. Suddenly, she is falling. I think she screamed. But it could have been the train whistle."

The man started whimpering again, reliving the moment, his shaky finger pointed toward the train depot in the distance, just beyond the glass towers.

"So, someone was with her?" Manning asked. "Could you make out who?"

He rattled his head. "So horrible ... horrible. She was so lovely..."

The man was beside himself. His legs gave way and he collapsed. Manning and Colefield helped him to his feet. The Lieutenant pulled a radio clipped to his belt and called for assistance. Within moments, the lower bridge door popped open. Two of the crew rushed over. They each got an arm around his waist, keeping the man upright. "Take him to sick bay. I'll look in on him shortly."

"Wait!" Colefield raised his hand. "Felipe, can you identify the person with her on the balcony? Could she have been pushed? Was it a man or a woman?"

Felipe started trembling. "It was a—" He seized up like he'd drunk hemlock at the sight of someone coming up from behind the deputies. Tongue-tied and frightened, he stared beyond them at a bold figure appearing through a cloud of dust.

"What is going on here!" the man's voice boomed authority.

Luis snapped to attention.

The broad-shouldered man radiated strength. His lapelled dark uniform gave him the appearance of being seven-feet tall.

"Captain..." the Lieutenant said. "These officers are from the River Patrol. They are investigating an incident that occurred across the river last night." The Lieutenant walked over and whispered something to his commanding officer, then stepped back.

"And what does this have to do with us?"

"They were hoping that one of the crew saw something."

"And did they?"

"Felipe, sir."

The captain stared at Felipe. "Is this true?"

Felipe was in denial now. "I saw nothing..."

"He is lying..." Luis said.

The captain faced the deputies. "He is very upset. What have you done to him?"

Colefield made no reply. Manning said: "He was cooperating until you arrived."

The captain again faced the cook. Using a softer tone, he asked: "Felipe, there is nothing to be afraid of. What did you see?"

Felipe refused to make eye contact or speak. His head just bobbled.

The captain lost his patience. "Take him away at once!" he ordered to the crew. "See that the burn on his hand is treated and then bring him to my cabin."

Luis watched the men drag Felipe away.

Colefield wanted to object but knew it was pointless. Manning crossed her arms and looked frustrated, too.

"Felipe is my wife's brother," the captain went on to explain. "He is old and gets confused. He has no wife and no children. All he has is this job and the crew like him.

Unfortunately, his memory is not good. He has been known to see phantoms and make up stories. I will talk to him again later and see if I can't get to the bottom of this."

"He said he saw a woman fall from her balcony and I believe him," Manning blurted out. "He is a viable witness. We'll need his statement."

"We will cooperate, but you have no authority over us in these waters."

Manning stepped closer. "We can make a call to the Marshall's Office and have this boat impounded, if that's what you would prefer?"

The captain glared at her. "Nonsense! Your threat is meaningless."

Colefield stepped forward. "Captain, Luis informed us you were not aboard when the incident occurred. Is this correct?"

"I turned the bridge over to Luis after we set anchor and returned to my cabin to rest."

"Luis mentioned that you took shore leave after you set anchor," Manning corrected. "Which is it?"

"That is true. After a brief rest, I left the ship at 2300 hours."

"Where did you go?" Manning pried.

The captain grimaced. "That is none of your concern."

Manning asked. "When did you return?"

"It was after midnight. I would have to look at the logbook to be more precise. It would be better if you let me handle Felipe. As I said, his health is not good, and his memory failing. I know him best. He will open up to me."

Colefield dug out his card and handed it to the captain. He seemed relieved and stuffed it inside his pocket without reading it.

"We are in port for a few more days. We'll be in touch."

Manning glared at him. "So will we…"

3

Across the river, Colefield still felt angry. He jumped off the bow, hit damp ground and his boots sank in a foot of soggy sand. He slapped the bow line around the same slab of concrete and stormed off toward the twin towers, leaving Manning behind.

In his head, he revisited what Felipe had told them. The fact that the captain felt he needed to control his crew seemed perfectly reasonable. Manning had not seen that. The poor cook acted as if he was having a stroke. What the hell had she been thinking? They needed the captain's cooperation if they were going to get a statement ... and they didn't need an international incident on their hands.

When he reached the towers, he glanced up at the top floors. Looking back at the ship's position, he did some quick calculations.

Just beyond the twin towers he noted the empty train depot. Then he heard Feinstein's voice in the distance but didn't immediately see him in the crowd. The body had been removed from the fountain. Uniformed officers trickled back to their vehicles. Reporters were packing up their equipment. The excitement seemed over, which suited Colefield just fine. He assumed the body had been loaded inside the ME's van and would soon be on its way downtown. He finally saw Feinstein up near the street, talking with an employee. The young woman held a large ring of keys at her side.

Manning caught up with Colefield. She grabbed his shoulder stopping him. Impressed with her strength, Colefield paused.

"The captain's a misogynist."

"These are international carriers. You need to tread lightly."

"You saw the look on the old man's face. He seized up as soon as the captain arrived. He knows something."

"I'm going to talk with Feinstein. Tag along if you want."

"Tag along? That's what I get, rank and file? Just for the record, I wasn't out of line. And why is the captain being so evasive on when he returned to the ship. Don't you find that a bit odd? We should have checked the logbook."

She was probably right. Colefield walked off. Manning followed him up the bike path toward the street, matching his pace, step for step. Feinstein was still carrying on a conversation when they approached. The woman with the keys appeared to work at the Condominiums. She had on a beige uniform with a WFPC logo over her left pocket. Her short blonde hair had a razor cut. She looked fit.

"Deputies, this is Blake Brighton, the concierge here. She was working last night. She believes the deceased is Kris Kerns. Ms. Kerns owns unit 801A, an upper floor condo in the North Tower. It has a walk-out balcony overlooking the fountain."

Feinstein turned and pointed out the luxuriously glassed unit. "What else can you tell us about her, Ms. Brighton?"

The concierge appeared controlled, unshaken by the recent news. She smoothed out one of her eyebrows and put on her best Mona Lisa smile. "She was very private," she said. "I didn't have much contact with her."

"Did she ever act depressed?"

"No, not really. As I said, she kept to herself mostly. You think she may have killed herself?"

Manning asked. "Did anyone visit her last night?"

"I would have to check the surveillance video."

"What about in the past, did she have many visitors?"

"A few. They may have been clients. I can't recall if I ever saw her with anyone special."

"What kind of work did she do?"

"She was a private investigator." Brighton checked her Rolex. "Detectives, I'll need to take the Medical Examiner up to the unit now. Can we continue this later?"

"Ms. Brighton," Manning said, "before you head off, Detective Feinstein may have asked this already but when was the last time you saw Ms. Kerns?"

"Wednesday. Around seven PM. She came up to the front desk and asked if she had any deliveries."

"How did she appear?"

"Calm, I guess. She always appeared together, in charge."

Feinstein cut in. "Did she have a delivery?"

"Yes — a large bouquet of roses."

"Who sent them?"

"She didn't say."

"Was there a card with them?"

"Yes."

"Do you know what florist delivered them?"

"They were dropped off by a chick wearing an Oregon Duck's cap. That's all I remember."

"Does the building have 24-hour concierge coverage?" Colefield said.

"Yes, sir, normally. But one of our concierges is out on pregnancy leave, so we are short-handed now. We only provide coverage from 7am until 11pm. That's just until Jenny returns in two weeks. Then I go back on the graveyard shift."

"When did you leave the front desk last night?"

"I shut things down at around 11pm."

"I noticed that there are two lobbies but only one concierge desk. Is that true?" Feinstein asked.

"Yes. The north tower lobby has no front desk."

"I noticed cameras on the perimeter of the buildings," Feinstein added. "Are there cameras inside?"

"Yes, in both lobbies and the parking garage."

"Not in the rest of the building?" Colefield asked.

"The board has discussed putting cameras in the elevators and stairwells but that has not been approved."

Manning cut in. "Has there ever been any break-ins?"

"We've had some cars broken into, but it's rare. I've never heard of a unit being broken into."

"I'll need to view the footage from last night," Feinstein said.

"Of course."

The ME and her assistant walked up. The ME had on a white blouse with water marks on it. She swiped her hand over her pants and shook Colefield's hand. Her male assistant shook Manning's hand. "Good to see you Colefield. You know Feinstein, right?"

"Yeah, we're old buds. Beverly Manning meet the State's best ME, Chris Carter."

"You mean the only State ME," she corrected, turned and shook Manning's hand. "Good to see a woman working River Patrol."

"It's only temporary, Ma'am."

"That's what Colefield said in the beginning..."

The ME shifted gears. She faced the concierge. "Shall we get the show on the road?"

"Yes, Ma'am. I'll take you up now."

The ME said to Brighton: "On second thought, you and my assistant go on ahead. I'll catch up with you."

The concierge hesitated, and then walked off with her assistant. Once they were out of range, the ME said to Colefield: "I've seen that look before ... something on your mind?"

Colefield chose his words carefully. "Was the victim sexually assaulted?"

"I'll need her on the table before I can answer that conclusively. There was too much blood to determine that without an examination. She died on impact. There's tissue damage at the center of her lower back and on both arms just above the elbows. Bruising mostly. May be related to the fall or something else entirely." She paused, motioning toward the concierge she'd be right along. Then she leaned over and whispered to Feinstein: "God I could use a smoke."

Feinstein pulled out his pack and offered her one.

The ME accepted it. "One of these days I'm going to have to quit these."

Feinstein lit it for her. She took four or five deep puffs and then stomped it out.

"By the way, deputies you're welcome upstairs, the more the merrier. Just give me time to grab a few samples and take some pictures."

"One last thing, Ma'am," Manning said. "We have reason to believe that someone else was on the balcony about the time of her death."

"We do?" Feinstein brow raised. "That would be good information to share."

"A witness from the ship made a loose statement," Colefield said. "We don't know how accurate it is."

The ME nodded and walked off. Feinstein watched her, clicking his pen, presumably thinking about what the ME had said about the girl in the fountain or what Manning was suggesting. He snapped out of it and looked back at the deputies. "Fill me in."

Colefield started to say something when Manning cut him off. "We weren't able to get the witnesses full statement because Colefield's a pussy."

Colefield didn't take the bait. "He may not turn out to be reliable. He's old and his health isn't good. We'll try again later."

"How'd the captain respond to questioning?"

"He and Manning didn't see eye to eye. I believe he'll cooperate, despite that."

"You two don't need to stick around. I'll take it from here."

Colefield shrugged and started to walk off. Manning dug her heels in and stared at him. "Aren't you the least bit curious to see inside her place?"

He remained neutral on the subject. Feinstein gave them a moment to work it out.

Manning didn't hesitate. She took off toward the lobby on her own.

Feinstein stuck his pen in his pocket. "She grows on you…"

"What are you talking about?"

4

After twenty-minutes inside the luxurious condo, they had more questions than answers, and very little to go on. There didn't appear to be signs of a struggle. The furnishings were modern and tasteful. Floor to ceiling windows, a built-in wine refrigerator stocked with some expensive brands, and a beautiful bouquet of red roses sitting on a glass end-table. In neither bathroom did they find any medications or other illegal substances suggesting she was self-medicating or suffering from depression. From documents found in her home office, Ms. Kerns held a law degree from Berkeley and was a licensed private investigator in the state of Oregon. She'd been working five-years as an investigator and had plenty of case files. No particular case caught Feinstein or the deputies' attention, with one exception, a file for the Port of Portland was missing. There was a slot for it in her filing cabinet but no file. What was also missing was what they presumed was her laptop. A cord was plugged into the wall, but the computer was gone.

Feinstein made some notes before he walked out onto the balcony and joined Colefield who was staring down at the fountain, thinking.

"Nice Place," Feinstein said, and tucked his pen into his shirt pocket. "If I need a new line of work, maybe I'll retire and become a PI."

"Doesn't seem worth it. Look what happened to Ms. Kerns..."

"You're probably right. What's your hit on this?"

"That she was pushed. But by whom, that's your job."

"C'mon, we're short staffed. Manning has ten years working the streets. And you're not so bad yourself. Don't throw in the towel."

"You're becoming very political in your old age."

"Follow-up and get the statement from the cook. Maybe it'll provide a lead."

"I'll see what the Lieutenant says."

"Now look who's getting political..."

Manning walked out onto the balcony and joined them. "Place is as clean as a cat's ass."

Feinstein chuckled, and put his notebook away. "I couldn't get anything out of your partner, what's your take on this?"

"It feels personal."

"One of her clients?"

"That or a jealous husband or wife. Some of those photographs were incriminating. Hell of a way to make a buck, peeping into bedroom windows."

"Infidelity must pay well." Colefield yawned.

Manning looked back at the bouquet of roses. "I say we start with the flowers."

Feinstein reached for his cigarettes then had second thoughts. "What do you make of the uniforms and hardhat in her closet?"

"Disguises," Manning said. "Look and act the part, you can blend in most anywhere. Maybe she was out snooping around some warehouse, trying to blend in, and somebody didn't like it so much. I'm anxious to look at the surveillance video."

"We'll do it on the way out," Feinstein glanced over toward the ship across the river.

Manning brushed some loose hair from her face and stared at Colefield. "Well, partner, what's your two cents?"

"That there's a million ways to die..."

Later, after they all viewed the surveillance video from the previous night, Feinstein stopped along the curb and pulled out a pack of cigarettes. "I'll be in touch, Colefield."

Colefield glanced over at the train depot, lost in thought.

Feinstein turned to Manning. "I'll work with the concierge to see if we can narrow down any possible suspects."

The two deputies said little on the run downriver toward the shed. Manning kept to herself, withdrawn mostly, manifesting the funk Colefield was exhibiting. Colefield was still ruminating on the gruesome image of the girl floating in the fountain and how fucked up it was.

They both eventually snapped out of it when they reached River Patrol Headquarters. Manning jumped on to the dock and secured the bow and stern lines.

Before they reached their office a slender man in a yellow suit and polished shoes stepped out of the shadows and approached them.

Colefield figured the guy was there to meet someone down at the marina, a yacht broker or potential client. Then he saw the gold detective's shield strapped to the man's belt and caught the tense look on his partner's face.

"That's close enough, Richard!" Manning snapped.

The man ignored the comment and continued toward them.

"Who's he?" Colefield stopped.

"My soon-to-be Ex."

"Need me to stick around?"

"I can handle the shit-bag."

The man laughed. "Doubtful, Bev," he said in a scratchy voice. "Now can we cut the crap?"

Colefield decided to hold his ground. Something about the man rubbed him the wrong way.

He was carrying a large envelope in his left hand, his other hand was down at his side, his gold rings glittering in the sunlight. A slight bulge under his jacket indicated he was packing a gun.

"What do you want, Richard!" Manning said firmly.

He stepped forward and handed her the envelope. "You can read the subpoena now or later. I don't really give a damn. Just wanted to have the pleasure of delivering it personally."

Manning threw it to the ground. "Fuck you."

He didn't seem the least bit affected by her outbreak. "I'll give you a heads up of what I'm asking for. The house and Roxy."

"Fuck if you get Roxy. She's mine!"

"Life's a bitch. See you in court."

The man started to turn. Manning grabbed her pepper stray from her vest, aimed it at him and fired.

"I told you to stay away from me, asshole!"

The man's reflexes were cat-like. Just a trace of the spray struck his cheek. He calmly used the back of his hand to wipe it away, glaring at her.

"That's going to cost you, Bev honey."

Manning stowed the spray and shoved by him. Colefield stared at the man's chameleon-like expression. It went from Mr. Nice to Mr. Hyde in a split-second.

Colefield bent over and picked up the envelope. "You dropped this."

5

He hadn't slept well and woke up early to a ringing cell. It was not the call he had been hoping for. He skipped the coffee and headed straight to work. Manning was already there. She had a latte in her hand and one just like it on her desk. As he came through the door, she handed him the second latte.

He took it, feeling surprised. "Thanks," he said. "What's the occasion?"

"Figured we got off to a bumpy start yesterday. Truce?"

"Sure. By the way, I never got a chance to ask you yesterday, who's Roxy?"

"She's my four-year old German shepherd."

"He's holding your dog hostage?"

"He's an asshole."

Colefield took a gulp of coffee. "Must be rough. Bart fill you in on the call we received?"

"Yep. I filled the tanks on the sled. We're ready to go."

"Let me hit the head first."

A half-hour later, their patrol boat pulled into a marina of houseboats off NE Marine Drive. Judge Brown lived in a luxurious two-story houseboat. The manager of the marina had not been around when it happened. If he had been, perhaps she would not be answering the door covered in blood.

She was shaken and bleeding from a head wound. She hurried the deputies inside and closed the door.

The white bathrobe covering her stout body had blood splattered down the front. Her forehead had a purplish inch-long gash. A wad of cotton was stuffed up one nostril quelling the bleeding there. She led the deputies into the main area of the houseboat.

Manning stared at the cut on her forehead. "Ma'am would you like us to call the paramedics?"

"I've called a friend. She'll be here shortly. Sit down, please."

"Elizabeth, what the hell happened?" Colefield hadn't expected to blare out his words, but they came from some deep place within.

"Excuse me for a moment," she said and hurried off toward the galley and opened a cupboard by the sink, removing a tall crystal glass. She poured a slug of vodka that would have impressed a czar and gulped it down. The drink stabilized her trembling hands.

Colefield looked around. He hadn't been in her home before but wasn't surprised that the furnishings looked expensive. Judge Elizabeth G. Brown was as tough as they came. Her family had made a fortune in the Oregon timber industry. She carried that same drive through the ranks, cut her teeth in the public defender's office before being elected.

She put the glass down and felt the pinkish skin around her nose. "Go ahead and look around. I've got to get this bleeding to stop. I'll be right back."

Manning asked. "Need any help, Ma'am?"

She disappeared down the hall without a response.

Manning wandered around the place, careful not to break anything, as if she was touring a museum. There was a life-size bronze sculpture in the corner, which caught her eye.

Colefield walked off in the other direction to examine the windows. They were intact. No signs of prying. The latches were secure. Nothing appeared to be knocked over, no broken glassware, furniture or vases. He went over and inspected the front door. Nothing jimmied or busted there either. All the paintings seemed to be in place.

When the judge returned, color was coming back into her face. She had changed out of the white terry-cloth robe and now had on a black one from the same designer and had washed off the blood from her forehead.

"I've checked the entire house," she said. "Nothing seems to be missing."

"We should probably collect the robe you were wearing," Manning said. "If there is any DNA on it, might help the DA identify your attacker."

"I'll think about that."

Colefield said calmly: "Can you describe who assaulted you?"

She looked him in the eye. "That's the problem."

"What do mean?"

"I didn't see anyone."

"You mean they hit you from behind?"

The comment seemed disorienting for the judge to process. Manning started to ask another question but Colefield stopped her.

"What can you remember?"

"That I woke up on my bedroom floor covered in blood."

She bent forward, recklessly picked up her empty glass, raised it to her lips, and then stopped, apparently forgetting she'd polished off the expensive Vodka, and put the glass down.

"Where exactly?"

"Upstairs."

"When?"

"Around 8 am..."

Manning frowned. "Without a description of the assailant there's not much to go on, Ma'am? Unless we can lift some fingerprints."

She glanced at the name badge on Manning's uniform. "Deputy Manning," she said with a moment of restraint. "I have been over it twenty times in my head. I must have been assaulted, but I can't provide a description or any evidence. The blood you saw when you came in is my only proof."

Colefield nodded to Manning. "Mind if my partner looks at your injuries?"

"Be my guest." The judge slouched back, tried to relax, but couldn't.

Manning removed a pair of nitrile gloves from her vest pocket, put them on, and began with the forehead and then moved to the scalp.

"Ma'am, there's no evidence that an object was used. It looks like it was caused by a fall."

Colefield didn't see any bruising around her neck or arms.

"The last thing I remember is turning the lights off. I usually double-check the doors and windows, make sure they're locked, before getting into bed."

Colefield thought for a moment. "Do you still live alone, Elizabeth?"

She nodded.

Manning asked: "Do you own a gun?"

"I send people to prison, deputy. I tend to be paranoid. I sleep with a Smith and Wesson under my mattress and a Remington in my closet."

"Do you have a housekeeper?"

"Yes?"

"Do you provide them a key or leave it under a flowerpot outside?"

"Did you see a flowerpot outside my door?"

"We're on your side here, Elizabeth," Colefield reassured her.

"I'm sorry. Of course, you are. Gracie has her own key. She cleans every week like clockwork. She's trustworthy."

"Who's responsible for the maintenance at the moorage?"

"A retired man named Fred Foster."

"Does he have a key to your place?"

"Fred repaired a faucet in the kitchen last month. He returned the key after the job was finished. Fred is trustworthy. He lives at the moorage; I've known him for years."

"Who owns the marina?"

"Eddy Markel — aka Big Eddy — and no, he doesn't have a key. We own our houseboats. We just pay him for the slips."

"Can you think of anyone else who might have a key?"

"An intern of mine had one. She used to watch the place when I traveled. But she's living out of state now."

He pocketed his notebook. "Mind if I look around upstairs?"

She rose slowly, rubbing her right knee as if it was sore. "Go ahead." She messaged her temples, slowly rolling her head back and forth. And then, something apparently triggered a memory, because she looked distraught.

"I always leave a window cracked for JC to go in and out as he pleases. I haven't seen her since last night."

"JC is your dog or cat?"

"A Manx. You didn't see her outside, did you?"

"No, Ma'am."

The judge walked toward the spiral staircase across the room.

Manning whispered. "Something is not right here."

Colefield looked as if he agreed. He caught up to the judge at the base of the stairs.

She asked: "Isn't your partner coming?"

"I want her to double-check downstairs first."

The upstairs was comprised of a large suite with an outdoor deck. The judge walked over to a sliding glass door, unlocked it, and slid it open.

The air outside smelled fresh with a hint of cedar. Colefield walked out onto the deck and looked around. He didn't see anything suspicious like a ladder propped against her roof. It was a good twelve feet drop and a good ten feet between other houseboats. Money could buy spectacular views, but it couldn't shield a person from criminals. They always seemed to worm into a person's life.

Down at the end of an adjoining dock, a heavyset man in overalls was down on his knees, sanding with an electric sander. He had a young helper, a scrawny teenager, who walked over to him, lugging a 5-gallon orange bucket filled with tools.

"Is that maintenance worker your guy, Fred?"

She turned and looked. "Yes."

"What about the kid?"

She stared. "It could be Fred's nephew. He mentioned he might be hiring someone for the summer."

"How about your neighbors? Any trouble there?"

She wrinkled her brow. "A few months back a sleazebag from California wanted to build another Trump Tower where you're looking. It would have blocked my view of the mountains. I flexed some legal muscle to get him to rethink his plans."

"Where's he now?"

"Gone."

"How much did it cost him?"

"Not enough for the aggravation he caused all of us."

"And this guy just walked?"

"Not at first. He wanted a buyout. He got it, essentially. But in the end, he had no choice. For the most part, we're a contented community here. A few riff raffs, some eccentrics. But that's par for the course. This lifestyle attracts artists and loners. It's why I like it here. It feels safe. Or at least it did."

"Could he be involved?"

"No. He's a slimy bastard but he got what he wanted and left town."

"Tell me about Big Eddy."

"He's a little odd, more money than brains really. I shouldn't say that. That was mean-spirited. He gives the place character and looks out for us." She pointed toward a flat-roofed blue and yellow trimmed houseboat seventy-feet away. A circle about three-foot round was painted on the roof. "He lives over there. The one with the drone landing pad on the rooftop. I thought at first he was a pervert when I saw his drone buzzing overhead with its Go Pro camera. That was before he saved JC from a hawk."

"Well, he didn't do such a good job of looking out for you today. Can he fly a drone here legally with the airport so close by?"

"He can as long as he keeps within one-mile of it and below the 400-foot height restriction. We're about two miles from the runway."

"Is there a possibility he may have recorded something?"

"I don't think he's here." She stepped out and glanced over toward the parking lot. "I don't see his Turquoise Eldorado. He leaves at the crack of dawn on Saturdays to get in line for Voodoo donuts."

"Anyone else come to mind?"

"If it's someone from the marina, I'd be surprised."

"You're sure of that?"

She shrugged. They went back inside.

"This has me rattled. I can't figure out what happened…"

"How would a jury look at it?"

That got her thinking. "I see your point. I'll try harder."

He looked at her bedroom and then went and peered inside the bathroom. There was one opened window above the hot tub, certainly wide enough for a cat to climb in and out but a person would have to be small. "Is this the only window you leave open at night?"

"We both know what I do for a living — I'm not a complete lunatic."

He moved on. He walked by a wall of large closets with brightly colored dresses, blouses, suit jackets, all organized by color with rows of shoes perfectly faced-off. Everything looked neat and tidy. If someone had been hiding in there, it didn't show.

She hadn't made the bed, probably left it how she found it. She wouldn't be one to disturb a crime scene. An empty brandy glass sat on the nightstand alongside a pair of reading glasses. On the opposite nightstand sat a stack of case files, some of them had sticky note tabs. Colefield felt underneath the mattress. He pulled out a Smith & Wesson, checked to see if it was loaded, then put it back.

A five-drawer dresser was opposite the bed. He would have kept an additional weapon in the second drawer from the top. It would be easier to get to in a pinch. But that was his line of thinking...

"What cases are you working on currently?"

"I'm due to rule on a rather important one. It's the mess with the Longshoremen's Union. I'd rather not go into it."

Colefield thought about the girl in the fountain. There were some files in her condo that indicated she had been interested in the union wars.

"This may sound like it's coming out of the blue, but do you know a woman by the name of Kris Kerns? She studied law at Berkeley U.C. Thirtyish, works as a PI here in town."

"KK?" the Judge exclaimed. "Yes, of course I know her. I knew her father very well. Old school. Real gentleman lawyer — dabbled in politics until his death. I had dinner at their home in the West Hills many times and attended KK's graduation. I offered her an internship, but she declined, said she didn't want to practice law. That she wanted to try her hand at something else. It broke her father's heart, but he didn't interfere. She is a strong person, determined, a class act really. She excels at whatever she sets her mind to…"

"You may want to sit down, Elizabeth. I've got some bad news."

She refused to sit, and her eyes darkened.

"My timing couldn't have been worse. We found her body yesterday. We think someone pushed her off her 8th floor balcony."

Distraught with the news, the judge flopped down on the edge of the bed, tears in her eyes. "She called me just last week. She wanted to get together to talk about this ordeal with the unions. I told her I couldn't because of my connection with the case. She told me she had some information that she had obtained from one of her clients that might be helpful. I warned her to be careful. All sides are angry. KK was always fearless. Same as her father…"

Colefield gave her a minute for the news to sink in.

"Did she mention this particular client?"

"No."

"I'm very sorry for your loss."

He gave her more time to absorb the terrible news. It was then that he saw the bloodstain on the rug beside her bed. It triggered a memory of the girl's blood in the fountain.

The stain looked wet. There was also a bloody handprint on the walnut bed post. He figured after she came to, she saw the blood on the rug or felt her bleeding forehead with her right hand and then used the bed post as support to stand up. It would be a normal reaction. The print was most likely hers.

He pulled out his cell, shot a few pictures of the overall bedroom and then snapped a few close-ups of the blood stains, before he put his cell away and jotted something in his notebook.

"Mind if I ask you a few more questions about what happened this morning. Were you wearing the bathrobe when it happened?"

She thought about the question before responding. "I put it on afterwards."

"Were you sexually assaulted?"

"No. I've been over this in my head ten times. It's one of the reasons I called you."

"Were you at work yesterday?"

"Yes."

"What did you do afterwards?"

"I left the courthouse around 6 PM. I had a cocktail at a local bar and came home."

"One?"

"Does anyone really just have one?"

"Then what?"

"Then I made some pasta, read some case files, watched a little TV and went to bed."

"Did anyone approach you at the bar?"

"Just the usual suspects. They're harmless."

"Did you receive any calls after you got home?"

"I don't think so. If the landline rang it did while I was in the shower. I can check for messages when we go downstairs."

Colefield heard Manning's boots thudding up the stairs. He lowered his voice and asked quickly: "Have you ever had a blackout, Elizabeth?"

She cocked her head. "What are you implying?"

Colefield met her cold stare. "It's just a question…"

"I'm not a drunk."

Manning appeared behind them, cuddling a black and orange spotted cat, which delighted the judge, and seemed to bring her some comfort following the horrible news.

Manning handed-over the cat.

The judge kissed its nose. "He appears fine. What a relief…"

Colefield put his notebook away. Manning met his stare and shook her head, indicating she hadn't found anything.

"Why don't we go downstairs to wait for your friend to arrive?"

6

The doorbell rang. Judge Brown put the cat down by her feet and started toward the door. Colefield told her to hold up. He walked over and peered out the peephole.

There was a woman outside. She had light brunette hair, wore blue nursing scrubs and carried a black medical bag at her side.

Colefield stepped aside. "Your friend is a nurse?"

"ER doctor."

The judge opened the door and the woman hurried inside.

"God, I was so worried, sweetie. I drove as fast as I could. Are you, all right?"

She led the judge over to the sofa where they sat down together. She gave the judge's hand an affectionate squeeze.

The judge turned and faced the deputies. "Deputy Manning, Deputy Colefield, this is Becky Irish."

"Ms. Irish," Manning shook the doctor's hand.

Colefield did so next. "Ma'am."

Becky had the confident look of someone used to dealing with crisis, which was reassuring. After introductions, she examined the judge, concerned with the bump on her forehead. She asked her to turn slightly so she could pull the collar of the bathrobe down to inspect her neck.

Colefield asked: "Where's your landline, Elizabeth? With your permission, I'd like to check if you received any calls last night?"

She nodded and pointed toward an antique table in the hallway. "Just hit the lower button on the right side of the phone. There isn't a password."

Becky reached down and pulled out a small handheld light from her bag and examined inside the judge's ears. "Well it doesn't look like you broke anything, sweetie." Satisfied, she put her light away and added: "Let's go into the bathroom. I want to look underneath your robe."

The two left. Colefield walked over and checked the telephone while Manning made a final pass of the kitchen. The message light was lit on the machine.

Colefield hit play. There was only one message that had come in two night ago. It was a woman's voice. "Elizabeth, it's KK, pick-up please ... I've got something important to tell you. OK. You're not home. Call me when you get this! It's very important..." There was a moment of dial tone before the caller hung up.

Colefield was thinking about the call.

Manning walked over and said quietly: "Think they're a couple?"

"That was a message from Kris Kerns."

"The judge knows her?"

"Family friend."

Before they could talk more, the doctor appeared. She said to Colefield: "She needs a few stitches which I can do. Everything else looks fine. I'll see that she gets an x-ray later. She also told me about KK. I'm going to give her a sedative and stay with her."

The judge lost in thought wandered out into the hallway. The doctor helped her over to the sofa.

"We'll take a thorough look around outside now, Ma'am," Manning said, as if she was trying to lessen the tension in the room, give the judge some space to grieve. "We'll speak with neighbors, see if they saw anything. If the manager of the marina is around, we'll speak with him too."

The judge said nothing.

Colefield gave her a moment and then asked: "You want us to send in a fingerprint crew?"

The judge shook her head. "No."

"We'll get to the bottom of this."

The deputies started toward the door.

"Colefield!"

He turned back. "Yes, Elizabeth?"

"Keep me informed on KK's case. Anything, anything at all that I can do, you let me know..."

"I will..."

Colefield walked over and handed the doctor his card. "If she remembers anything, call me."

7

Colefield was trying to make sense of it all while he and Manning walked among the houseboats banging on doors.

Manning finally asked: "Why'd you tell her?"

"In our line of work, certain connections are inevitable. I didn't have any idea she knew her. But once I found out, I didn't want her learning about it from some damn newspaper. And we learned a valuable piece of information about Ms. Kern. That she called the judge with questions about the Longshoremen's Union and ICSTI, just before her death. The judge also informed me that she is getting ready to rule on the case. Call me paranoid, but there's a connection."

They weren't having much luck rousting neighbors. They stuck business cards in several of the doors and then finally gave up and went to speak with the maintenance man and his nephew.

Fred slowly rose and brushed dust from his knees. "Going to be another hot one..."

Colefield nodded. "Mind if we ask you a few questions?"

"Ricky, why don't you gather up the tools while I talk with these deputies?"

The boy stashed his cell in his pocket and let out a sigh.

The man said: "Let's go talk over there in the shade."

They moved under the awning of an old houseboat and sat in some cheap deck chairs. Colefield gave the man a minute to pull out a pack of cigarettes before he started with the questions.

"What's on your mind, officers?"

"I'll get right to it," Colefield said. "We have reason to believe that Judge Brown's houseboat was broken into this morning."

Fred's brow crinkled as he fumbled to light his cigarette. "Ms. Brown? She OK?" The man seemed genuinely upset by the news.

"She'll be fine."

"What happened?"

"She was assaulted."

"By who?"

"She never saw them," Manning said.

"But she's going to be OK, right?"

Manning nodded. "We don't have much to go on." Colefield looked back toward the judge's houseboat.

"You have any idea who might want to harm her?" he asked.

Fred took a long draw from his cigarette and shook his head.

"We understand you did some plumbing work for her. Did anyone else help you with that job?"

"Come to think of it, I did hire a guy to help me out on a few jobs. But I don't think he was working for me then. I returned her key. Only had it a few days…"

Manning asked: "What's your relationship to Ricky?"

"He's my nephew. He's staying with me for the summer. My sister thinks it's good for him to learn a few carpentry skills. He needs discipline. After his parent's divorce, he had a little run-in with the Law."

Colefield raised a brow. "How long ago was this?"

"Six or seven months back."

Manning scratched her nose, staring over at the skinny boy. "What'd he do?"

"Shoplifting. He's in those awkward teenage years where we don't always make the best decisions."

"Does he ever enter any of the residents unsupervised?" Colefield asked.

"We always work together. But I keep an eye on him. I trust him. He's working out some issues but who hasn't at that age."

"What about other residents down here..." Manning said. "Know of anyone who might have a grudge?"

The man blew out a lungful of smoke. "Nope."

Colefield figured Fred was the ears and eyes of the moorage. If anyone knew something, it would be him.

Fred scratched his shoulder. "Have you spoken with Big Eddy about this?"

"Not yet."

Fred checked his wristwatch. "That's right. He doesn't usually get back here until the afternoon."

Colefield pulled two cards from his wallet and held them out. "If you see Big Eddy, give him my card and have him call me. You care if my partner asks Ricky a few questions before we leave?"

"Go right ahead."

Manning left, talked with the boy for a few moments, and then returned, shrugging her shoulders. "Zip..."

Fred reached down and ground his cigarette out in a rusty coffee can. "I should get back to work."

"One last question. Can you vouch for Ricky's whereabouts last night?"

"He was home with me."

"What about this morning?"

"I woke him at seven-thirty for breakfast."

"That does it then. Well, thanks for your time."

8

Colefield set *The Oregonian* aside and poured himself a second cup of coffee. There had been no follow-up on Kris Kerns' story, and given what he knew, he figured the editor was doing his homework. Either that or someone was putting pressure on the newspaper to keep her story out of the headlines. There also had been no mention of the Judge's incident in the newspaper and that didn't surprise him. Elizabeth would never agree to talk with a reporter. His office had done their part, kept the assault quiet, as she had requested. He had not received a call from her or her friend, Becky Irish. The event was still a big mystery.

He still felt irritable and pensive, and he figured, although he didn't want to admit it, that it had something to do with Jill being out of town. She had gone back East to see her parents and he had missed her calls and hadn't been able to connect to find out how things were going. His girlfriend had left two messages, but they revealed nothing. It sounded like she was under stress but couldn't talk.

He made a move toward the refrigerator for some almond milk for Calico Jack — stretched out on the windowsill in the warmth of the morning sun — when his cell rang in the other room. He hurried over and answered it, hoping it might be her. But caller ID indicated it was from First Alert.

"When did this happen?"

"Would you like us to dispatch medical help?" The operator said. "That's our usual protocol."

"I'll call you right back." Colefield hung up, took a big gulp of coffee, before charging out the door.

After fifteen steps or so he barged inside his landlord's houseboat.

"Bill!" he shouted. "Where are you?"

He heard a noise upstairs.

"I'm up here, Old Boy!" Montgomery said and coughed. "Would you be so obliged to give an old fart a hand?"

Colefield weaved through the dirty dishes in the galley and climbed the spiral staircase to the upstairs area. The large room had the usual military clutter spread out everywhere. Stacks of old New York Times, a cache of gun magazines, a collection of pearl-handled knives, antique swords and other oddball stuff, along with a canopy king-size bed, Montgomery's throne. The blankets were thrown aside. Colefield remembered a recent hot tub incident when he'd been summoned by the same emergency service. He found Montgomery on the floor unconscious and bleeding from a nasty cut on his forehead. His date at the time had said Montgomery slipped climbing out of the hot tub, cracked his noggin on the floor, all in a semi-drunken state, and was unconscious. The sixty-seven-year-old art collector looked shaken, shivering and dripping wet, wrapped in a beach towel, aghast that her Don Juan may be dead.

"Where the hell are you?" he called out.

"Johnny's in the john. I've fallen and can't get up!"

Montgomery was sprawled out on the floor by the toilet, his sweatshirt pulled up over his stomach, his pants around his ankles, his underwear twisted in a knot. A phone receiver dangled from a cord on the wall just inches above his head, a constant beeping irritation.

"Kill this pesky device, will you!"

Colefield reached in and hung up the receiver, and then bent down and examined Montgomery's extremities.

"Is it your left leg? Is it broken?"

"No — my spirit is."

"Seriously, Bill..."

"I'm being serious."

"Focus on your appendages."

"It's the left hip. It's out again."

"Can you sit up?"

"Better not."

Colefield hit redial on his cell. He told the operator the paramedics would need some device to get a one-hundred-eighty-pound former marine down from a second-story bathroom. They'd never finagle him down the narrow spiral staircase; they'd have to bring him down another way....

"Tell them to bring their tethers. They'll know what you mean." Montgomery rolled his head up off the floor and grinned. "This might put a crimp in my sex life..."

"How bad does it hurt?"

"At my age, a little pain is a good sign. Nothing a decorated Marine can't handle."

"Want me to call your son?"

Montgomery grimaced. "I'd prefer a shot of rum."

A few long moments passed in silence before Colefield heard sirens in the distance. The EMTs were near. "Don't go anywhere."

"So, you're a comedian now?"

Colefield went downstairs and opened the front door. Four firemen, seasoned in rescue attempts, tromped in lugging harnesses, ropes, and medical equipment.

"He's upstairs."

"No worries, gent," one of the blond-headed paramedics said with an accent. "We've whittled the lad out of logjams before."

"He's conscious."

"Is he tight?"

"Stone cold sober."

"He's a jolly nipper. Don't mind his banter one bit."

The men trekked up the stairs in single file. Colefield kept his distance, figuring he'd just get in the way. The telephone rang downstairs. It echoed through the house. Colefield answered it.

"Hello! Is this William?" The female caller asked.

"No. Is this Ms. Ashlee? It's Jason Colefield."

Sally Ashlee was one of Bill's old flames. "Is William all right? I received a call…"

"The paramedics are here with him and I imagine it's going to be the same drill. They'll probably take him to Good Sam. It's his hip again."

"I'll check on him later at the ER. I'm glad you're there." The line went dead in his ear before he could respond.

Two of the EMTs came down the stairs empty-handed and headed toward the door.

"We're getting the litter. Need to isolate the pelvis before we move him."

"How does it look?"

"A little elbow grease and maybe the doctor will be able to pop it back in place. It's above our paygrade or we'd do it. You a neighbor?"

"Tenant."

"Lucky you."

Later, Colefield stood in the salon area beside the stairs out of the way of the paramedic handling the stabilizing rope from downstairs. The other EMTs were lowering Montgomery over the edge of the balcony. A stabilizing rope was attached to keep the litter from swaying too much.

"Colefield, Old Boy. You down there?"

"What do you need, Bill?"

"Are you getting this on video?"

"You're not going to make a YouTube."

"It does wonders for pity fucks. Get the camera…"

Colefield followed the men out to the ambulance. They loaded Montgomery in back and asked if Colefield wanted a ride to the hospital.

"Are you taking him to Good Sam?"

"Yep. Same as last time."

"I'll notify his son. Thanks for taking such good care of the old coot."

"Our pleasure."

Montgomery rolled his head. "Can't hear ya, but I'm all for ya…"

9

Colefield arrived to work late and before he had time to settle in the Lieutenant called him into his office. "How's your landlord?"

"They took him to the ER. It's his hip again."

"My dad's the same way. Bad joints take a man down faster than a bottle of Jack Daniels."

The lieutenant checked his watch. He had on another tight-fitting button-down shirt. The snug collar looked like it was cutting off the circulation because his cheeks flushed when he stood and the pudginess around his middle caused his shirt to come untucked.

"What are you doing here on a Sunday?" Colefield asked, glancing down at the Lieutenant's cluttered desk.

"Too much going on to take the day off. Any more news on the girl in the fountain?"

"Nothing."

"Keep me posted."

Colefield returned to his work area. Two desks with computers were empty. A third was occupied by Deputy Bart Ryan, who was on the telephone, jotting down information on a yellow pad. Someone needed River Patrol to help a stranded boater just south of Tomahawk Bay. Colefield hadn't worked with Bart in about a week and missed it. Manning was OK, but he had a special liking for Bart, more a mentor role than he got with Manning.

Speaking of Manning, she walked through the door looking ready for action.

She had on regulation black shorts, a short-sleeve shirt that had a few buttons undone at the top, and a light-duty tactical vest for holding mace, flashlight, several 40-caliber magazines, and a two-way radio. All the deputies had identical vests but hers looked more organized.

After Bart was done on the telephone, he leaned back in his chair, smiled at Manning, got up and walked off.

The Lieutenant made a half-ass tug on his collar and tucked his shirttail in. "I'm off to meet with the mayor. The Longshoremen are threatening to strike again Monday. The mayor thinks he can head it off but still wants to brief me in case shit hits the fan."

Colefield realized he was staring at Manning's chest, lost in thought. He snapped out of it. "When will Weaver be back?" he asked the Lieutenant.

"He's got the newbies out on a training exercise in the 32-footer? Could be an hour or more."

"Lieutenant — I filled out the paperwork you asked for," Manning interrupted. "Should I hang onto it for now?"

"Drop it on my desk. I'll sign it when I get back."

The Lieutenant flew out the front door. Colefield heard the dull roar of the cruiser fire up in the parking lot. He sat down at his desk, turned on his computer and sensed he was being watched from across the room.

Manning was staring at him when he turned.

"If you're bored, head out with Bart."

Manning dropped her paperwork on the Lieutenant's desk and sat down, reading emails on her cell.

"You finish your report?"

She looked up, frowning. "It's in your inbox."

"When did you type it?"

"Last night."

"I thought you were off today?"

"I need the overtime. Lieutenant Luis called this morning. Two interesting things came from our talk. Felipe is reneging on his story. No surprise there. Claims he imagined it all. Second thing, the ship's captain is missing. No surprise there either..."

"How long?"

"Left Saturday and hasn't been heard from since. I told you he was guilty."

"When are they scheduled to leave port?"

"Three hours ago."

"You're sure the ship is still here?"

"I saw it from across the river an hour ago."

"You went back to the towers?" Colefield sounded surprised.

"Drove by after I tracked down the company who delivered the flowers to Ms. Kerns." Colefield remembered the bouquet of roses at the crime scene. "The florist provided the name on the order. A Diego Rafael. Turns out it's our missing captain."

Colefield was impressed. Maybe he had been wrong about things.

Manning stood, seemed eager to get wet, began bumping Colefield's chair with her shoe. He finally got up, press checked and holstered his Glock.

"Let's go pay Luis another visit."

* * *

Seagulls scavenged food along the shoreline near the grain elevators now sitting silent. No workers hustled along the docks or operated cranes, or pumped grain into the ship's hull. The area was quiet except for the idling engine of the River Patrol boat, gliding up to the *Piranha*.

A deckhand walked out and tossed a rope ladder over the side of the ship. It slapped the water with a bang that sent the birds screeching into flight.

Colefield killed the engine and followed Manning up the ladder. From mid-ship he glanced back over at the two towers across the river, thinking about Kris Kerns, her bloody body lying face down in the fountain. Her death seemed so removed from the calm river and the morning sunlight reflecting off her building now.

The deckhand was patiently waiting to take them to the bridge. Manning rubbed her palms as if they were sore from the climb. "Has your captain returned?"

The deckhand shook his head.

"Any idea where he might be?"

"No, ma'am."

"Is this your first time to Portland?"

"No, ma'am."

"What about this ship, first time aboard it?"

"Eleven time."

"Does the captain often go missing?"

"Never missing but he leave sometime. But never this long…"

They headed toward the bridge. When they entered, Luis was standing with another officer in a white uniform. He turned, attempted to smile, then walked over and shook hands.

"I am glad you are both here," he said. "This is most unusual. We are late leaving port and another ship is scheduled to arrive tomorrow. But we cannot leave without our captain."

Manning seemed like she was looking for the right words to say, so Colefield jumped in. "How long have you known that your captain was seeing Kris Kerns?"

"Who is this?"

"The women pushed from her balcony…"

Manning added: "Consider your answer carefully, Lieutenant."

Luis looked at his crewmates. "Would you please give us a *momento?*" He gestured for them to leave the bridge. After they were gone, Luis said: "The captain is a very private man. I just learned of this liaison."

"Really? I find that hard to believe," Manning said.

"Is the captain married?" Colefield asked.

"He has a wife and two children back in Panama."

"Does he have a lady at every port of call?" Colefield asked.

"He has never neglected duties aboard in the five years that I have served under him."

"I'll take that as a yes. Where do you think he went?"

The Lieutenant said nothing.

Manning pressed him. "We have a dead girl on our hands and now your captain is our number one suspect. We need to find him."

"He is no killer."

"His disappearance suggests otherwise. We know he visited her condo on the night of her murder. Your cook confirmed it."

"He did no such thing."

"I saw the way he trembled when the captain began questioning him. The man's eyes couldn't lie, even with a gun pointed at his back. The fact that you say he has no memory of the event now is a blatant cover-up. We need to speak to him."

"He has been quarantined to sickbay. No visitors. Captain's orders. We cannot afford to spread a disease to the other crew."

"What are you talking about?" Colefield asked.

"He is very ill."

"That's convenient," Manning uttered, not believing a word of it.

"It is not convenient. We have no one to cook us meals. We will have to live on rations until he is well enough to work again. Perhaps you would like a temporary job in the kitchen?"

Colefield tried to calm the situation. "What's wrong with him?"

"Our medic believes it is the measles."

"It's not life threatening."

"For someone his age, it is."

"OK — Luis," Colefield said. "We'll leave. But when we find your captain, you'll all have some explaining to do.

You may want to call your shipping company and tell them you're going to be delayed."

10

After they left the ship, Colefield decided to head over toward the twin towers. He idled along the shoreline, near where they had tied off the day of the crime. He told Manning to keep an eye out for anything in the grass or along the water's edge.

"Did you buy his story?" she asked, her intense eyes combing the riverbank.

"None of it."

She glanced back at him. "At least we agree on something. What are we looking for exactly?"

"The missing laptop or file. How long were you married?"

The question surprised her. "Where'd that come from?"

"Any kids?"

"Just Roxy."

"Why'd you volunteer for River Patrol?"

"I needed a change. You OK?"

"Change is good."

"You're starting to sound like my soon-to-be Ex."

"I'm only an asshole on occasional. Any more trouble with him?"

Manning's expression turned cold. "With Richard, trouble is his *modus operandi*..."

An object in the water ahead caught Colefield's attention. He pointed it out to Manning but by then they had idled past it. He circled the boat round so they could take another look. It turned out to be nothing — just a hunk of plastic, some junk washing ashore. He had hoped it might be the laptop, because whoever killed Ms. Kerns had probably stolen it, wanting to hide evidence. That seemed clear or they wouldn't have left the cord behind. Whatever was on her laptop must have been damning. But to whom? The captain? The Port of Portland? The Longshoremen's Union? The operators of Terminal 6?

Manning pulled out her cell. "Feinstein should know the captain is missing."

Colefield put the boat into neutral to keep the noise down. "Ask him if he's had any hits from the security footage."

Manning dialed Feinstein and spoke with him. When she was finished, she slipped the cell back into her vest pocket. She faced Colefield and the sunlight lit up her face, turning her skin golden brown. He'd never noticed how attractive she was. He felt an attraction and told himself to knock it off.

"What'd he say?"

"He's working with the concierge. They've narrowed it down to a few visitors that could be possible suspects."

"That's progress..."

"Remember the person in jeans, a Nike t-shirt, and a baseball cap pulled down low, blocking their face from the cameras? Feinstein ID'd him. He works for the Port of Portland, upper echelon of Port activities. He's going to visit him later today. See what he can find out."

"Anyone else?"

"The Pizza delivery kid, freckled, red hair, bulky — actually, a younger version of you."

Colefield looked down at his flat stomach. "Bulky?"

Manning grinned. "OK — broad-shouldered."

Colefield almost laughed. "What about him?"

"He's clean. No connection to Ms. Kerns. He was delivering pizza to a neighbor."

"Who else?"

"The concierge ID'd another man. She believes it's the captain."

"What took her so long?"

"Good question. She remembers him from about two months ago. I guess he's a regular. Shows up when his ship is in town. Why she didn't tell us earlier is too fuckin' bad for us. We could have taken him into custody Friday."

"Who arrived first?"

"Pizza guy. Then the person in the baseball cap. Then shortly after, the captain."

"So he was the last one to be seen with her ... that doesn't bode well for him."

11

They spent the rest of their shift trying to track down the captain with no luck. Colefield said he had to visit Montgomery, which was true but when he got caught in heavy traffic on I-5, he said to hell with it and took back streets home.

The next day he showed up for work feeling a little hungover. He and Manning had been busting ass and pulling overtime and dealing with their own shit. Unless they turned up something soon, the case would be dead in the water, and Colefield didn't want that to happen.

He shoved some paperwork into his desk drawer and told her he'd see her in a few hours, leaving the office around noon. He drove his truck across town fighting heavy traffic and finally arrived at Good Sam. The old Ford was steaming from under the hood when he parked it in the underground lot.

The receptionist at the front desk said that Mr. Montgomery had been moved from ER to Short Stay on the 3rd floor.

"Room 306. Take the elevators…"

Colefield didn't really listen to her last comment because he'd visited his landlord too many times to count and knew every nook and cranny of the medical center. It was a training hospital so there were plenty of younger doctors and students running around all the time that kept things interesting.

Bill's door was open, and he had his own room. He was sitting upright, watching TV, IV lines stuck in both arms. His blue gown was open in front and electrodes were hooked to his chest. He rolled his eyes toward the door. Colefield had a gut-wrenching thought. Perhaps this could be him one day.

"Why Colefield old buddy," he said, hoarsely. "Good to see you lad. Break me out of this joint, would you? It has no hooch."

"How are you, Bill?"

"Middlin' to shitty. Nothing a good shot of Pussers wouldn't fix."

"They realign your socket?"

"Boy did they … now I want to realign them! Bastard hurts!"

"What's with all the electronics?"

"Hell, they want to check out my ticker. Guess its running a bit slow. What do they expect from an 85-year-old?"

"So, they're keeping you overnight again?"

"And not even providing me any female companionship."

Colefield walked over to the side of the bed and glanced out the window. The view was adequate — a neighborhood view of quaint NW homes along Lovejoy with a few small taverns he'd frequented just around the corner.

"You need anything?"

"A get out of jail pass would be nice."

"I'll see what I can do. Have you called your son?"

"Good god, no. He's off in the outback of Alaska. He doesn't need to know any of this."

"If you're not out by tomorrow, I'm calling him."

Before Montgomery could argue, a friendly-looking female doctor walked in wearing scrubs with a stethoscope slung around her neck. She had light brunette hair and green eyes. She looked over at Colefield and smiled.

"Hello again, Deputy Colefield. Is this handsome devil a friend of yours?"

It took Colefield a second to place the face. "Becky Irish. How's everything?"

"I'll let you know in just a minute—" She turned and faced her patient. "Well, Mr. Montgomery, have you been behaving? You were pretty agitated a few hours ago."

Montgomery batted his eyes at Ms. Irish like she was the finest thing he'd set eyes on since Playboy.

"My, what a lovely dish," he said. "Are you here to bathe me?"

"Afraid not," she stepped up to the bed, removed her stethoscope, stuck the ends into her ears and pressed the large bell against Bill's bare chest and listened, moved it back and forth a few times and then stood back. "Well, you're alive, that's a good thing. How long has your pacemaker been in?"

"Oh, dear, that would give away my age."

Colefield added: "Looks like he's smitten."

"Well, I'm going to speak with your last surgeon and see what he recommends. I'll be back is there anything you need?"

Montgomery smiled. "Just more time with you."

Becky grinned at Colefield. "Could I speak with you in the hall for a moment?"

"Sure."

Colefield glanced over at Montgomery who was blowing kisses toward Becky as she walked toward the door.

"I'll check on you later," Colefield said. "Behave."

Montgomery shooed him away.

Out in the hall, Becky was looking upset. Her features had hardened and Colefield figured whatever was on her mind wasn't good.

"I'm worried about Elizabeth," she uttered. "Have you heard from her? I've been trying to reach her all morning. She told an assistant she was heading home. That was an hour ago. She's not answering her cell or her home phone."

"Maybe she got caught in traffic?"

"No, I don't think so. She's been acting differently these last few days. She's not herself."

"She's probably still shaken. First, her possible break-in, and then learning of her family friend's murder. I'm sure it has her rattled."

"Rattled, I understand. This is something beyond that."

"I'd be happy to make a welfare check later today. Can I reach you on your cell later?"

"Yes, I'll leave it turned on."

"I'll check in with you when I get there."

"Fair enough, and thanks."

"Happy to do it. Is Mr. Montgomery going to be OK? It's hard to get anything out of him."

"I'll check in with his regular doctor. We want to monitor his heart for 24-hours and see if we need to alter his medication to increase his heart rate. There is a slim possibility we may have to go in and replace the pacemaker. I'll keep you in the loop. Does his next of kin live in the city?"

"No. He's got three children. His two daughters live in Washington — one doesn't speak to him. The third, his son, is a fishing guide in Alaska. I suspect he's out in the bush and out of cell phone range. He had an older brother who passed recently. Bill is taking it hard. They used to have lunch together at the Mac Club every Wednesday."

"Call me, please — just as soon as you locate Elizabeth."

12

Manning's jeep was still in the lot when he pulled into River Patrol Headquarters. The cruiser and the 4 x 4 were both gone. Manning was alone in the office, listening to the marine radio while cleaning her Glock on her desk. There were a few scribbles on a yellow pad nearby. She had metal parts strewn everywhere. A pistol cleaning kit was open. A red shop rag and a can of CLP were within reach. She sneezed, swiped at her nose, and picked up the can of gun cleaner. She looked over at him.

"Hey, Colefield — how's the landlord?"

"They're keeping him overnight again for observation. Where is everyone?"

"Bart and Weaver took the recruits out to Lemon Island. A call came in that some nut job is running around naked threatening to kill himself. The deputies thought it would be good training." She picked up a cotton wad and sprayed it with CLP. "Oh — the Lieutenant called. Things are heating up at Terminal 6. He may need us to run a sled down there later if the protests escalate."

Colefield sat down. "You got a smudge on the side of your cheek." He pointed to it, but she ignored it for the moment.

"Before I forget — you got a call from Jill somebody. She said you'd know who it is. She wants you to call her at this number in New York." Manning set the can of gun cleaner down and picked up a yellow sticky note and handed it to him. An oily thumbprint was pressed right down in the center of the 10-digit phone number and Colefield had difficulty making it out.

"This isn't her cell. You sure you got it right?"

"Yep."

"How long are you going to be?"

"Ten minutes, tops. Why?"

"We need to do a welfare check on Judge Brown."

"If she's up to it, I'm going to ask her some hard questions about Ms. Kerns."

"You like to burn bridges, don't you?"

"Not particularly. But we're at a dead-end, unless Feinstein comes up something. I didn't sleep worth a shit last night. I kept seeing her body in the fountain. I want to know if she was having an affair with the captain..."

Colefield went outside to place his call to Jill in private. He stood alongside the building and stared over at The Sextant, the restaurant she owned. He imagined her there, slinging drinks behind the bar, in that sexy red top, those tight white shorts, and tall turquoise cowboy boots. He wished she'd never gone back East to visit her parents. He hadn't been himself since she left.

After six rings his call went to voicemail. It was an older woman's voice, not Jill's spritely tone. Colefield assumed it was her parent's phone but why she wasn't using her own cell puzzled him. He left a brief message that he'd try again later.

When he reentered the office, Manning was slipping her freshly oiled gun into its holster. She'd wiped the smudge from her cheek. "Ready when you are."

The white rolling wake from their patrol boat disappeared into the distance. It was a beautiful time to be on the water. Sun was bright and warm. The mild breeze blowing straight down the gorge, smelled like the desert. Sailboats were out in force: their mainsails, jibs, and spinnakers flying brilliant colors of the rainbow. Powerboats roared past with skiers in tow. Sandy beaches overflowed with sunbathers and families crowded around picnic lunches. Yet, for Colefield, the beauty seemed to reinforce his sense of isolation.

Manning glanced over at him and broke his funk. "Jill your girlfriend?"

"Something like that."

"Not much of an answer."

"It's an honest one," he said and pointed out over the bow. "There are shallows ahead. Keep to port."

Colefield glanced toward Lemon Island as they made their way down the narrows, just a spit of land and trees and sand, but didn't see the familiar green-hulled patrol boat. He figured the deputies had taken the northern channel or were tied up on the opposite side of the island in the narrows. For an instant, in one of the small coves, he thought he saw a familiar old sailboat loaded down with jerry cans, outboard engine parts, and clothing drying in the wind, but it turned out not to be the old River Rat he remembered so clearly from July. Just a mirage. An illusive fabrication, given life by a memory of a case that turned out OK in the end....

The memory faded when the houseboats of Elizabeth's marina came into view. Manning began a broad turn toward the dock. As they approached a seagull squawked a warning cry from atop one of the pilings and a few Mallards swam out of the boat's path as they glided to a stop.

They tied off and climbed out. Manning took a few steps and stopped, pointing up at something black, zipping by in the sky. The small drone circled back, hovering over them briefly, before zipping off and landing on a rooftop at the end of the row.

Manning laughed. "Big Eddy must be home."

"We're going to pay him a visit afterwards."

The deputies walked down the ramp passing by the maintenance man's houseboat. His gangly nephew was on the deck sipping a Coke and staring at them as they passed. Fred was nowhere in sight.

Next, they ran into a very excitable, short man, wearing a Hawaiian shirt and flip-flops heading their direction. Not an inch over 5-feet, as round as tall, wispy patches of dark hair flipping around in the breeze. His prized possession, the remote control for the drone, hung at his side like a six-shooter.

"Big Eddy at your service, deputies. How may I help?"

"Relax. We're here to visit the judge," Manning said.

"Let me take you to her." Big Eddy was a man with a purpose.

"We know the way."

"No trouble at all. Was just finishing up my afternoon patrol, you might say. Excellent way to keep an eye on things, never know when some riff raff might sneak in. Not you two of course..."

"Did Fred give you my card?" Colefield asked.

"What did you want again?"

"Have you seen any strangers around the marina in the last few days?"

"Not a one. And my eyes in the sky would know. I upgraded the camera to a super resolution, ZX6 model. Nothing gets past old Big Eddy — ask around. Before drones, I had cameras mounted everywhere. Kind of an electronic freak, you'd say. But a secure marina is a safe marina, right officers?"

Manning cracked a smile. "Can't argue with that B.E."

"B.E! Oh, that's precious."

Colefield said: "Have you seen the judge today?"

"No, sir. Odd, too. Her car is in the parking lot."

Colefield nodded to Manning and they moved along, Big Eddy insisted on leading. He walked heavy-footed and tended to sway with each step, more of a waddle than a walk. The three of them stopped at the judge's door and Manning did the honor of knocking.

The door wasn't completely latched and swung open.

Colefield saw groceries lying on the floor, then he saw the body. He drew his Glock and charged in. Manning signaled to Big Eddy to stay back, drew her weapon, and went in next.

The judge wasn't moving. She was down on her side, blood dripping from her nose. One of her heels had fallen off. Groceries were scattered along the floor. Colefield's first impression was that she had been jumped from behind.

He scanned the interior, nodded for Manning to search the rooms, and then bent over and checked the body for a pulse.

It was faint, her skin warm to the touch. Thank god, she was alive.

Manning gave an all-clear for the downstairs and Colefield led the way upstairs, Manning following behind. Following a quick search of the area, nothing looked out of place or disturbed.

Colefield holstered his Glock. They went back downstairs. Big Eddy was trembling in the doorway, staring at the body on the floor, his skin pale and clammy, too shaken to come any closer. Colefield thought he might faint.

"She's alive," Colefield told him. "I don't believe she's seriously injured."

Big Eddy let out a heavy sigh and then screeched as the judge's tabby darted through his short legs and ran inside the house. Manning started for her gun and then stopped.

Colefield squatted down beside the judge and examined a small laceration above her right eye. He didn't see any blood on her scalp or major bruising. He pushed some hair back from her face and her eyes shot open and she bolted upright.

"Take it easy, Elizabeth. It's Colefield." He steadied her.

She was groggy but recognized him.

"Do you need me to call an ambulance?"

She looked surprised by all the groceries lying on the floor. "What the hell happened?"

"I was hoping you could tell us."

"Ms. Elizabeth, dear, what on god's earth happened?" Big Eddy shouted from the door. "Were you attacked?"

Manning walked over to him, whispered something and then closed the door.

"I'm fine, deputy," the judge said. "Really, I am. Confused as all hell, but I don't need medical attention."

"We'll get you fixed up."

"What happened here?" Manning asked.

The judge cringed. "Looks like I fell and hit the floor. I didn't see anyone. I can't say with any certainty if I was pushed from behind or not."

"What do you remember — was your door locked?" Colefield asked.

The judge reached over and grabbed her Coach handbag off the floor. She looked inside it. Her red wallet and Prada sunglass case were inside as was more of her personal items but there was no keyring. She then felt underneath her skirt, as if something was poking her, and held up a set of house keys.

"I must have had them in my hand. I remember my purse was slung over my shoulder and I was juggling the sacks of groceries. I sat one down and opened the door, and then I kept my keys in my hand, picked up the sack of groceries and walked in. That is my last memory."

"We found your door unlatched," Manning said.

The reality settled in her troubled eyes. She began trembling. Manning grabbed a throw blanket from the sofa and wrapped it around her shoulders. Colefield felt the judge's forehead. It felt damp, clammy feeling. "Get her some water," he said.

Manning went into the kitchen and Colefield heard her going through cupboards.

"Take it easy, Elizabeth. Let's get you to your feet and move to the sofa. Can you do that?"

"Don't baby, me." She tossed the blanket aside and started to stand.

"I'm going to call Becky Irish now."

"She'll worry."

"She already has been."

"I'm either losing my mind, Jason, or someone is stalking me."

Colefield held onto her until she was stable on her feet. She was a little shaky at first but then straightened and seemed to find her bearings. He helped her over to the sofa and she sat down. "I'm going to go get you a washcloth, it looks like you scraped your eyebrow and bloodied your nose."

"Oh, crap, not again! This is getting tedious."

Without a second thought, she swiped the back of her hand under her nose. The bleeding had stopped but there was a smear of dried blood on her hand.

Colefield went into the bathroom, found a washcloth in a drawer, held it under the hot water faucet for a moment and then carried it back and handed it to Manning. The judge looked down at her glass. "Colefield, be a hon, and throw a little vodka in that for me. The bar is behind you."

"Just as soon as I call Becky."

"She'll be upset; I know her…"

"She has good reason to be."

Colefield walked across the room and made the call. Becky Irish said she had another round of patients to visit and then she'd be over to stay with her.

"What happened exactly," Becky asked, before he hung up.

"She doesn't know. We found her unconscious on the floor."

"I'm so worried this involves one of her cases."

"Has she mentioned something to you?"

"No."

"I'll ask her."

"Thank you, Deputy."

He put his cell away and then rummaged around the bar for a bottle of Vodka, found a partial bottle of Grey Goose and carried it over to the table.

He started to pour a shot in her water glass, and she stopped him. She took a big chug of water first and then held her glass out.

"Top it off."

While Colefield filled her glass to the brim, she said: "My father died from liver cancer when he was 66. I never knew him not to have a drink in his hand. I learned some bad habits at a young age."

"Those were different times," Colefield said.

"Not so different ... oh, I've got something to show you." She gulped some Vodka, put the glass down on the table, and looked over at the mess on the floor. "One more favor," She pointed to her handbag. "Grab my purse and bring it over."

"Hold still," Manning said to her, lifting the washcloth. "I'm near your eye."

"Pour a little Vodka on it. Best antiseptic I know of."

Before Manning could object, the judge grabbed the washcloth from her hand, doused it with alcohol, and handed it back.

Manning just shook her head. "You're pretty good at getting your way," she said.

"You don't know the half of it."

Colefield fetched the purse and carried it back over and set it down on the table. The judge wasted no time rummaging through it until she found what she was looking for. She pulled out a sheet of yellow paper, handed it to Colefield. On it were several handwritten names.

They meant nothing to Colefield.

He showed them to Manning, who shrugged. He handed the paper back to the judge.

"Keep it," she ordered.

"What's the significance?"

"One of those bastards has to be the person stalking me."

"Elizabeth — we haven't found any proof you're being stalked."

"Aren't my injuries enough?"

"You know what I mean," Colefield said.

"Look at me. I'm collecting scars and lumps like a prize-fighter. It's one of them. They all made threats at one time or another. They're all out of jail now and on the streets. Two were released a few weeks ago — Susy Q Stanton and Peter Fink. I sent Susy Q away on prostitution charges twice. The last time she got out, she ran back to her old pimp and started turning tricks again. That lasted a few months and then she got pissed off at him. She didn't like giving freebies and bit a chunk of his penis off, spit it out the car window. The pimp pressed charges and had a very good lawyer. Susy Q got 18 months. She's pissed at me for not being more compassionate. She claimed it was in self-defense. Blames me for having to serve time again. Fink robbed a convenience store. He spent several years in county because of me. Thanks to overcrowding, he was released early, along with Susy Q and a cauldron of other criminals, by the liberal dumbasses downtown. The other name on the list is Robby Hanson a real gem, too. Assault and robbery mostly, he's been out of jail a month or more. He particularly holds a grudge because I sent his younger brother away on manslaughter charges while he was incarcerated, and their mother OD'd. He's probably got it in for me. It must be one of these scumbags. I could go on, but my hunch, it's one of them…"

"Let's go through the routine again … tell me what happened after you left work today."

"There's nothing to tell. I left the courthouse around lunch time, walked over to Nordstroms and returned a jacket I purchased last week. After that, I did a little window shopping, had a cup of coffee at Starbucks, then drove to Fred Meyer's on Interstate, and bought a few groceries."

"Did you have your cell with you?"

"Yes — oh, shit. I forgot to turn it back on. I had it off for a meeting."

Colefield looked at Manning. "That explains why Dr. Irish couldn't reach her earlier." Colefield looked back at the Judge. "No other stops?"

"Scouts honor."

"Traffic bad on I-5?"

"Isn't it always?"

"So that places you back here, say when? Four? Four-thirty?"

"Closer to 5…"

"And you didn't see anyone following you?"

"No."

"Your attacker was either in the house or they came up from behind when you had your arms full of groceries. If robbery was the motive, we don't see anything missing. If they wanted to do you in — why didn't they? Do you want to look around, see if we overlooked something? Place appears the same as when we were here before. It's got us scratching our heads looking for answers."

The judge glanced at her precious paintings and artifacts but said nothing while her cat rubbed up against her leg. She leaned down and picked it up off the floor, stroked it a few times, gave it a kiss on the nose.

"I'll go take another look upstairs," Colefield said. "Maybe we missed something."

Manning sighed. Mothering the judge was not her idea of fun. "What should I do with this washcloth?"

"Oh, deputy, just carry it into the kitchen. And, if you wouldn't mind, check JC's food bowl. I'm afraid to do it for fear if I bend over, I might pass out."

Colefield wandered upstairs and snooped around. He checked the windows, found a bathroom window ajar but the balcony door was latched. He went out on the roof-deck and looked around.

The marina had some activity — a few barbecues smoldering, people strolling home from work, and the drone was back, hovering over the judge's house. Colefield walked over to the ledge. Big Eddy was proudly perched on his roof, operating the controls.

Colefield looked over at the maintenance man's house and noticed Ricky sitting under the awning staring at him.

Downstairs, Colefield checked his watch. He figured Dr. Irish would be arriving soon and made a few observations in his notebook and then returned to Manning who looked pained opening a can of tuna fish on the kitchen counter. "I'm going to put a bullet in my head," she muttered.

"Not into domestic life?"

"I got nothing against cats, but this is $7-dollar Wild Caught Albacore."

"Let's go talk to the neighbors, then see if Eddy has any footage from today that might help."

The judge rose to use the bathroom. They kept their voices down. Once she was out of earshot, Manning said, "Twice now, and there's not a shred of evidence of a break-in or that she was assaulted beyond the small cuts and slight bruising, which could have been self-inflicted."

"You think she's staging it?"

"Do you?"

"You saw the list of possible suspects."

"She's reaching... If someone is breaking into her house, they're not leaving any evidence behind. If their motive is revenge, we would have found her beaten or dead. I think the woman is nuts."

Colefield snapped a few pictures with his cell of the mess on the living room floor and then shoved the groceries back into the two bags and carried them into kitchen and placed them on the counter by the refrigerator.

Down the hall, the door to the bathroom finally opened and the judge walked out, made no comment about the room being tidied up.

"Promise me, Jason," she uttered. "Take that list of names seriously."

"Give me a few days. I'll see what I can dig up."

After they left, Manning seemed in a hurry to get back to the Patrol Boat.

"Hey — hold up," Colefield said, heading toward a neighbor's door. "Where are you going?"

"If you think we'll learn anything from the neighbors, you're crazier than she is."

"When I went upstairs, I found a window open, but her balcony door was locked."

"And your point?"

"She may be your friend but she's a lush. This won't be the last time we pay her a visit. Mark my words."

13

Colefield figured Manning needed to blow off some steam. Letting her take the helm also gave him a moment to revisit what they had to go on: A list of three felons, a teenager with a petty theft charge who acted a little weird. No physical evidence. Perhaps they were missing something...

It was time to pull out his cell and go through the names on the list. He tapped into the county's court records and discovered they were a rotten bunch. Everything the judge had said appeared true and then some — assault, weapons charges, robbery, bribery, forgery and fornication. Their records ran the gamut. Not the types you'd want to take home to meet your mother.

It was a wild shot, but maybe one of them had connections with the Longshoremen. Maybe they hired one of them to frighten her, provoke her to swing her ruling in their favor. But wouldn't they have threatened her first? Left a clue? Made some gesture of future harm?

Before long, he lost interest speculating. The image of the dead girl floating in the fountain nagged at him. There was a connection. The judge had indicated she knew KK. Indicated she may have been working on something related to the union wars. Then there was this new list of criminals to add to the three suspects in the girl's murder: a Panamanian ship captain now missing, a stranger no one could seem to identify and a pizza delivery person. No physical evidence, except for a security tape that any good lawyer could get thrown out of court. The case made about as much sense as a judge claiming to be assaulted by phantoms. Had the cook on the *Piranha* also seen phantoms that night? Perhaps that's why Feinstein was dragging his feet. Yet Colefield was certain the old man saw something that put the fear of god in him. What if he had seen his captain push the girl over the balcony as Manning believed? Spilling that to them or his crewmates would be a nail in his coffin. The crew would surely have their revenge if he talked, because they seemed to like the captain. And all the old man had was ship life. It rang of desperation and isolation. Something that hit a cord within him.

Before he knew it, they were approaching Terminal 6, and Colefield snapped out of it. He'd almost forgotten Manning saying they were heading there instead of returning to the shed. The Port Authority landmark loomed on the horizon. Its size was astonishing — a full city-block long with seven monstrous cranes and an enormous dock for loading and unloading cargo containers. For as far as he could see nothing but thousands of shipping containers, lined, stacked, and waiting. A Hanjin cargo ship sat idle at the dock. This being the major hub for shipping for the Port of Portland and the entire Northwest, the facility looked incredibly bleak with inactivity. None of the cranes or the forklifts were moving. There were no workers or semi-trucks parked in long lines. Most of the railcars sat empty. It was one enormous cluster-fuck. And in the middle of it all, union protesters, shouting demands, waving signs, barking like rabid dogs. Perhaps a hundred or more — the International Longshore and Warehouse Union local 8 (ILWU) on one side and the International Brotherhood of Electrical Workers (IBEW) on the other, with ICTSI, the terminal operator stuck in the middle. Two labor unions and management locked in a stalemate. Each shouting and accusing the other of incompetence, worker slowdown and deliberate acts of malfeasance.

There was a small army of police in riot gear, on stand-down mode at the main gate, just waiting for the command to charge in, if all hell broke out. Downriver, a 25-foot, Defender-class Coast Guard vessel, waited. Manning looked as if she was going to piss her pants with excitement.

"You see the Lieutenant or the Mayor anywhere?" Colefield asked.

"My guess, they're holding a private meeting, with city officials, miles from here, negotiating with union bosses. My dad and I used to discuss this. He was a strong advocate of the unions but disagreed with their tactics on this one. I've been following this conflict from the beginning. It's been going on for years. It finally came to a head this week because ILWU wants jurisdiction over two jobs, plugging and unplugging reefer containers. See them over there? Those refrigerated shipping containers? The International Brotherhood of Electrical Workers (IBEW) has been doing the job since the 1930's. Now, the Longshoremen want the job, but the terminal operators aren't going along with them."

"When you worked patrol, did you ever get called out here?"

"Several times. Having this terminal sit idle ... think of the farmers and trades impacted by this petty bullshit. Those cranes should be operating round-the-clock."

"Did he support you being a cop?"

"Dad? Yes and no."

"He get along with your ex?"

"He thought he was scum. I should have listened, but I was too horny and naïve. So, what are we going to do here?" Manning cinched down her cap.

"See if you can get Bart or Weaver on the radio. Ask them if they've heard from the Lieutenant."

Manning reached for the radio mic and then froze, staring toward shore.

"Colefield look behind you!"

At the end of the dock, several of the protestors threw down their signs, pulled one of the opposing members out of a small group and pitched him off the dock into the water. The other side reacted by pushing and shoving before they began striking each other with signs.

"Oh, shit! Here we go…"

The flood gates opened and in came the riot police.

Another man was tossed off the dock near where the first man went in. Both were splashing about, trying to keep their heads above water.

"Let's get 'em…"

Manning steered the boat toward the men, idled up close.

"Give them a broad birth," Colefield said. "I'll grab the Shepard's pole."

Manning drove the boat perfectly. Colefield swung the pole out over the stern and the first swimmer got his hand on it and was pulled in toward the boat. After Colefield got him aboard, he went for the second swimmer and snagged him just as he was about to go under.

Once he got the second man safely inside the boat, Colefield pulled out some blankets from storage. He turned back around only to find the men at it, fists flying wildly.

One of them shouted: "You're an asshole. You're the cause of this!"

Manning stepped away from the helm and grabbed the loud one. Colefield got the second man under control but not before a wild fist clipped his chin. The man's big ring tore open his skin, leaving a nasty two-inch gash.

Colefield threw cuffs on him and pushed him down into a seat. Manning cuffed the other guy and kept him on the opposite side of the boat.

"You OK?" Manning asked.

"Peachy."

"Is it broken?"

Colefield glared at the guy that hit him and rubbed his jaw. "I don't think so."

"Your bleeding pretty good. Let me get the first aid kit."

Colefield swiped his arm over the cut. "Later. Let's get these two bums ashore."

14

After the deputies turned the men over to the police, they started to walk back to the boat, then overheard the men arguing again. One of them shouted: "Brighton! You prick!"

Colefield snapped round, told the officers to hold on, told Manning to wait while he walked over toward the men.

"Which of you is Brighton?" he asked them firmly.

The guy with the fat ring looked at him. "Yeah — I'm Frank Brighton ... what of it?"

Colefield studied the guy's facial features. He had the same Slavic nose and unmerciful eyes. His hair was light brown. Their had to be a connection. "You related to Blake Brighton?"

"Yeah — why?"

"Daughter, cousin or niece?"

"Daughter. She in trouble?"

"No— Are you with Union local 8?"

"Damn straight."

Colefield glanced at the other guy. "How 'bout you?"

"Same as that prick, Frank."

"I should have hit you harder!" Frank Brighton snarled and remained indignant. "Next time ... asshole."

Manning walked over for backup. "What's the beef, you two? Aren't you on the same team?"

"That dick is sabotaging everything, aren't you Brighton, go on, tell 'em. Be a man for once."

"Get him away from me."

"Deputies — this thing blew up when Brighton got seniority. All he does is add gasoline to the fire, don't ya, prick?"

Frank Brighton twisted out of the officer's grip and lunged at the other man. The two officers yanked them apart, got control of the situation again, and moved them away from each other.

"Take 'em away officers," Colefield said. "I've heard enough."

Manning stood her ground, watching the crowd slowly thin out. She tucked the back of her shirt in and waited until the officers loaded the men into separate police cars.

"Blake Brighton's dad is a Longshoreman," she said. "Now that's a strange coincidence..."

After mooring, they went inside the dark River Patrol headquarters and turned on some lights. Colefield shed his vest, slung it over the back of his chair and then went into the restroom. He left the door wide open and looked at his cut in the mirror before he began to run some warm water in the sink. He was looking for a washcloth when Manning walked in with a first aid kit, set it on the counter, and sighed.

"Let me look at it," she said.

Colefield turned off the faucet and faced her.

"It's nothing. I've been hurt worse shaving."

"Tough guy all the way, huh?"

"Go start on your report."

She refused to leave, crossed her arms and stared at him. "Don't pussy out on me."

"You're going to watch, that it?"

"I don't have anything better to do."

"Write your report. And while you're at it, write mine..."

Manning finally cracked a smile. "I'm going to stay here until you get the wound clean and then I'm going to put some antiseptic on it and if you wince, I'll let everyone know you're a pussy."

Colefield disregarded the comment and washed his face. He toweled it dry and then faced her again. "OK, mommy, fix me up."

Manning removed the antiseptic ointment from the first aid kit and then moved in closer. Unscrewing the lid, she looked as if she was about to squeeze out a big glob, then stopped. She looked Colefield straight in the eye. As if it was the most natural thing to do, she leaned in and planted a kiss on his lips.

It came as a disturbing surprise. Not because her lips didn't taste sweet or the kiss hadn't been sincere, but he felt emotionally drawn in. No longer was there this coldness clawing away at his soul. Just that fast, he'd been drawn into her web of charm like a Black Widow's fatal bite. It took every ounce of willpower to pull back, not take her up into his arms, plant her on the ledge of the sink, tear off her panties, spread her bare legs wide open, and have her.

She leaned back on her heels and slyly smiled at him. "Guess I was out of line, wasn't I?"

"Yeah."

"Won't happen again."

"Good."

She tossed him the tube of antiseptic and walked out of the room. Moments later, while he dabbed the ointment on his cut, he heard the office door close and her jeep start up in the parking lot. He put the medicine down and walked over to a window that looked out toward the street. He saw Manning, inside her jeep, the interior light on, using the rearview mirror to wipe tears from her eyes. When she finished, she straightened, repositioned the mirror, and instinctively looked his direction. As if she sensed someone was staring...

15

Manning had the next two days off for personal reasons, the Lieutenant told him. He figured there might be some fallout from what had happened, but his boss made no comment on it. It was just a kiss out of the blue, nothing life-shaking. That's what he'd been telling himself.

He'd spent those two days catching up on paperwork and making calls. He'd made a call to Luis aboard the *Piranha*. The captain had not returned, nor had they heard from him. Luis was getting heat from Hanjin. They were really behind schedule. A replacement captain was in the works, so they could leave port. After he hung up, Colefield dialed an old buddy at the Marshall's office and explained the situation. The Marshall's office agreed to pay a visit to Luis and impress upon him Colefield's concerns.

Montgomery was out of the hospital back in his houseboat and Colefield had been checking on him regularly, even sharing a few rums with him after work. He had not heard from Becky Irish or Elizabeth and he assumed that had to be a good thing. There was still no progress made in the case of the girl in the fountain. He ran a check on the concierge's father and confirmed he was with Longshoreman's union and had been arrested and released two other times for assault. The DA on both occasions threw out the charges. No one gave a shit if you got in a bar fight if you didn't kill someone. Hitting a cop probably wouldn't rank up there high enough to land any serious jail time. DA's were swamped with cases more serious then this one. As it turned out, Frank Brighton didn't even spend the night in jail. He was charged and released. Even so, he figured news would get back to the concierge about the arrest. He'd tried calling her at work, but she wasn't around. How she'd take the news, didn't really matter. Unless, there were things she wasn't telling them about the night of the murder.

Feinstein called bright and early Thursday morning and wanted to meet.

Colefield was happy for the break. He jumped in the cruiser and drove to the Pearl District, climbed out and stared over at the glass Twin Towers. A few blocks away he saw Feinstein's sedan parked along the curb. He crossed the railroad tracks and headed toward it.

He figured he still had time to try Jill again. He reached into his pocket, pulled out the crumpled scrap of paper with Manning's oil-smudged fingerprint and made a mental note of the number. Holding the paper got him thinking of Manning ... almost seemed strange not having her around the office and out on patrol.

"She grows on you..." Isn't that what Feinstein had said?

It rang twice before Jill picked up. "Where have you been?" he asked. He regretted the comment immediately, and stopped along the sidewalk, so he could focus on the conversation.

"In hell. Thanks for asking."

Her response struck a nerve. He felt disgusted with himself. "You OK?"

"For starters, I had my purse stolen and I had to cancel my credit cards. Seems I can't get a new passport until I have some identification. I spent yesterday trying to get a copy of my birth certificate while my mother bitched nonstop about the asshole my father's been lately."

"That pretty much sounds like hell."

"Oh, yeah, and my assistant manager called last night to let me know our new-hire has been pinching from the till. She had to fire her. Now, my bank account is overdrawn and two of my suppliers are threatening to stop deliveries."

"Anything I can do? And why do you need the birth certificate again?"

"So I can get an ID to board the plane."

"Tell me where it is, I'll be happy to overnight it to you."

"I've handled it. I don't mean to be a bitch. That was nice of you to offer. I'm just stressed out now."

"When are you coming home?"

"I don't know." She said irritably.

"I see…"

"Mother is listening. She is a snoop and I don't want her knowing my business. Jason, please, I can't talk now. How are you? Do you miss me?"

"Yes."

"It doesn't sound like it in your voice."

He couldn't win. "When should I call back? Now is obviously not a good time."

"I'll call you. Tell me you miss me."

His throat felt dry suddenly. He coughed. He started to speak but apparently Jill had heard enough, and the line went dead.

Nice job, Colefield, he thought as he hit redial. This time, she didn't answer. It went to voicemail. He gave up.

He walked over to Feinstein's sedan and climbed in the passenger door. Feinstein finished his cigarette and pitched the butt out the window. When he turned back around, he seemed amused by Colefield's injury. "You take up boxing?"

The deputy remained withdrawn, thinking about Jill.

"Don't keep me in suspense…"

He just blurted it out. "Manning kissed me. Jill knows. I'm fucked."

"A lot of drama for just a kiss. Did you tell Jill or are you assuming she knows?"

"She knows something's off. I heard it in her voice. We just got off the phone."

"So, you kissed your partner, big deal. You could do worse..."

"You're starting to sound like my shrink."

"Occupational hazard."

Colefield frowned and stared out the window. "It's like she intuits when I stray."

"Did you stray?"

"It was just one kiss."

"Let it go. If you're feeling guilty don't do it again. If you're not, then maybe you'll need to have a serious chat. For what it's worth, dating cops doesn't work. I speak from experience..."

Feinstein lost interest turned and pulled something from the backseat. He dropped a busted laptop onto Colefield's lap.

Colefield perked up. "Missing laptop?"

"A passenger on Amtrak's Cascades spotted it. He told the conductor. Conductor figured he had to tell someone. The girl in the fountain made the paper. He read about it. Since the computer was found across the street from the crime scene, on a hunch he called us. I had the good sense to run it for prints. Turns out it's hers. Unfortunately, the hard drive is ruined, and we turned up no other prints."

Colefield returned the heap to the backseat.

"I can think of easier ways to destroy a laptop," he said.

"My bet is they knew the train's schedule. Whoever killed her is methodical and smart."

"Why not just throw it in the river?"

"What if it floated? Or was found later? The hard drive would have been intact."

"Sure. But they took a risk being seen. Or what if the train was late and a homeless guy stumbled on to it on the tracks?"

"Union Station was convenient."

"So are a hammer and a dumpster."

"If you say so."

"Did I mention, Jill's purse got stolen in New York?"

"What's she doing there?"

"I told you last week, visiting her parents."

"Manning's got you distracted."

"There you go again, sounding like my shrink."

"Want to help me with this case or not?" Feinstein raised a brow and waited for his reply.

"You ID the guy on the footage?"

"Matter of fact, we have. You watch news on T.V. Colefield?"

"Just football. News is too depressing."

"I spent the last hour with the man in the video. He called our office when the story broke. Just like the conductor did. He works for the Port of Portland. He's Superintendent of Terminal Operations. I agreed to keep his name out of it for the information he provided."

Colefield picked at his cut. "Go on, you've got my attention."

"He visited Ms. Kerns house the night of her accident. He went there to pay her for some information. He hired Ms. Kerns to investigate rumors that someone from the Union Local 8 was sabotaging operations, causing work to slow down, which created a problem for the Port. He gave her an envelope of cash, because it was supposed to be under-the-table, discreet, not disclosed or leaked out later to the press. The Port is already taking heat for the strike. They want it to go away. If she found out who the players were, causing the slowdown, maybe they would have some leverage to use against the union bosses. It goes to the top."

"Sounds like motive for murder."

"He swears when he left, she was fine. Although she seemed in a hurry to have him leave."

"What sort of information did she provide?"

"She gave him a flash drive. It was supposed to have photographs and her findings on it."

"And it didn't?"

"It was blank."

"Which may explain why the computer was destroyed."

"That's right."

"Not very professional of her. The Port must be pissed off."

"Except she left a message on his office phone that she had made a terrible mistake and that she would bring the correct flash drive by his office the following day. So he thought things would be kosher."

"I need a beer."

"It's ten in the morning," Feinstein said.

"And your point is?"

"Keep what I told you close to your vest. And let me know if you find the captain. He's the last missing piece."

"Not so fast — I've got a little favor to ask." Colefield pulled out the list of names the judge had given him. He handed it to Feinstein. "Know any of these felons?"

Feinstein glanced at the names. "This have something to do with Ms. Kerns?"

"No, Judge Brown."

"She's a lush, you know. She's walking a fine line..."

"She is also about to rule on if the ILWU Local 8 violated federal labor law. She also knew Ms. Kerns and received a call from her the night of her death." Colefield went on and told him the rest.

Feinstein digested the information and reached for his cigarettes, then changed his mind. "You were going to tell me this when?"

"I'm telling you now."

Colefield nodded toward the paper, indicating he wanted the detective to take a closer look.

He glanced down at the list again.

"Show me faces to go along with the names, maybe I can remember someone."

Colefield had downloaded some old mugshots to his cell. He showed them to Feinstein.

"I've seen the girl around. I'd check with Drugs and Vice."

"I'd prefer to leave them out of it."

"What about Manning? Has she seen the list?"

"Roger that. Didn't recognize anyone."

Feinstein shook his head.

"Sure, you don't have time for a beer?"

"Will you get out of my car..."

16

The Dockside on Front Avenue had a fair-size crowd of old regulars and a few new professionals who lived in the condos being built in the neighborhood.

The place reeked of history. Before it was the Dockside, it was a restaurant known as "What's Up Doc?" And before that another restaurant called "Dot's Sternwheeler." Before that, it may have been used as a commissary for train workers. Best guess, the building was constructed around 1925. The exterior and interior looked constructed from lumber salvaged from pirate ships. It gave it bucket-loads of charm.

There were no empty booths or tables and only one seat vacant at the counter. Fresh brewed coffee wafted from the kitchen. A light had burnt out on one of the neon beer signs hanging on the wall but there were plenty of other B & W photographs and maritime artifacts to keep Colefield busy.

He flopped down at the counter next to a woman with her back to him reading a newspaper, a half-eaten plate of breakfast at her side. She wore tight-ass blue jeans and her dark hair cascaded down over her shoulders. She seemed to be ignoring the chattering of the customers and the clanking pots and pans from somewhere in the kitchen.

Counter space was tight. He sandwiched himself in and bumped the shoulder of the woman sitting next to him. She lowered her newspaper and faced him.

They were both surprised.

"Colefield, what are you doing here?" Manning said.

He regrouped. "No good morning kiss?"

Colefield noticed her dark eyes were a little bloodshot. "Rough few days?"

"Never marry a cop." She put her newspaper aside. "So, do we need to clear the air here?"

"Forget it ever happened."

"Done," she said.

"I got a call from Feinstein. We hooked up at Union Station. Turns out, he recovered the missing laptop."

"Excellent." Manning perked up and seemed genuinely interested. "Where?"

"Railroad tracks across the street from the Twin Towers."

"What'd they find on the hard drive?"

"A train had its way with it. There's nothing left but junk."

"You're fuckin' kidding, right?"

"Wish I was. But it gets better…"

"You're just filled with surprises this morning." Manning sat up straight.

The waitress came by with a fresh pot of coffee. She dumped a menu and coffee cup down on the counter in front of Colefield, filled his cup without asking if he needed cream, and then refilled Manning's and moved on.

Colefield lowered his voice. "Turns out Feinstein spoke with the other guy in the video. He works for the Port and hired Ms. Kerns to get some dirt on the Local 8."

He filled her in on what Feinstein shared with him, let her mull over the information while he took a sip of strong coffee — the perfect antidote for squelching the desire for a morning beer.

"The Dockside doesn't seem like your kind of hangout."

"What's not to like about this place?"

"I take you for a bran and yogurt girl. Not a trucker's breakfast."

"Fuck you," she said, but grinned anyway. "If you really want to know, I thought the captain might show up here."

That impressed Colefield. He hadn't counted on that. "Looks like he's our prime suspect now."

"He was banging her… something went amiss."

Manning stood up, pulled out a twenty and tossed it down on the counter. "See you at the shed…"

17

Colefield caught up to her outside the restaurant climbing into her jeep.

"Hey, Manning!" he shouted. "Hang on."

The jeep had its top off and windows rolled down. A pair of dog tags hung from the rearview mirror. She closed the door and waited. Colefield jogged over.

"Forget your wallet?"

"Take a ride with me. There's something I need to do before I head to the shed."

She looked at her watch. "Hop in. My jeep has a better stereo."

Colefield gave her directions. They drove down Front Avenue listening to Bluesville on Sirius XM. John Nemeth's "Feeling' Freaky" came on. Normally, he would have dug the sexy lyrics and bluesy harmonica but with Manning so close, it felt strange, like there was a message there. When they eventually turned onto Macadam, Manning broke the silence.

"I can't sleep lately," she said.

"Yeah, me, too."

"We're kind of a fucked-up pair."

"Speak for yourself."

"My ex is holding my dog hostage. How fucked up is that?"

"I'll have a talk with him."

"You don't know him."

"I'll get him to see the light."

"You're about to make me cry, asshole."

He pointed out the traffic light ahead. "Cross the Sellwood Bridge and make your first right. You'll get through this..."

"I wanted to believe this relationship was going to be the one ... and it turned out to be just the same as all the rest."

Colefield coughed. Her words hit a deep cord. Maybe he was just reading too much into Jill's silence.

He pointed where to turn. "Follow Harney Street down to the moorage."

They parked near the ramp leading to the houseboats. Manning killed the engine and started to get out. Colefield reached over and affectionately touched her on the shoulder. "I'll get your dog back, don't worry." He climbed out. Manning grabbed her keys and followed him.

They walked down the steep ramp, hopped over the gap in the catwalk, and took the narrow walkway to Montgomery's. Colefield banged hard on the solid oak door and then pushed it open and went inside.

"Who goes there!" boomed Montgomery's gravelly voice. "Intruders will be shot."

"Bill — it's me, Colefield."

"Colefield Old Boy, you're just in time," he looked up from reading his newspaper in his tattered bathrobe. "And I see you have brought a lunch guest."

"Beverley Manning allow me to introduce you to my landlord, William A Montgomery, Captain USMC, retired."

Manning nearly stumbled over some trash in the galley as she made her way over to the where Montgomery was sitting in his wheelchair. Montgomery dropped the paper and reached for his cane. He wanted to stand to greet the deputy.

"What a pleasure," he said and hobbled to his feet. They shook hands. "Why are you hanging around with such a rogue?"

Manning smiled. "We work together."

"Are you working undercover, dear? I like your outfit."

She laughed.

Bill took his cane and knocked a stack of newspapers off one of the cluttered chairs. "Have a seat, my dear." She sat next to him and became fascinated by all the targets stapled to his walls and ceiling. Then she looked at the endless old photographs, newspaper clippings featuring Montgomery in one situation or another, and locked on a framed metal hip socket from one of his many surgeries. "I call this wall my memoriam. A tad sentimental, but it's usually good for a little nookie."

"You've got quite a place here," Manning focused on one of the older black and white photographs of Montgomery in his Marine Corp days, holding a crumpled-up parachute after a jump.

"Too many times falling out of the wrong end of a plane caused that," Montgomery said, pointing his cane toward the hip socket. "The things we do for God and Country. Now tell me about yourself Ms. Manning. Have you been working with Colefield long? He has been keeping you a secret…"

Colefield cut in. "Bill, we're pressed for time. I need a favor. Colefield walked over and showed him the list of names that the judge had given him.

"See what you can find out about these felons. And do it as soon as possible, if you can."

"What's your hurry, Old Boy?"

Colefield glanced at Manning, who took the hint, and stood. He said: "If we could stay, we would. Think you'll have something for me by tomorrow? I know you have friends in low places … you won't find this group hanging out at the Mac Club."

"They look harmless enough?"

"Be careful. They're slimy and dangerous."

"That's my specialty. Fear not, Old Boy." Montgomery laughed. "I shall slither through their lives like a water moccasin."

Manning took another good look around at all the mermaids, swords, statues — the unique collection of artifacts the old pirate had collected over the years.

"It was nice meeting you Mr. Montgomery," she said and tip-toed by the various paperbacks, stacks of *Soldier of Fortune* magazines and yellow tablets scribbled with notes lying everywhere.

"Come back when you can stay awhile," Montgomery said to her. "We'll share some champagne and lies..."

18

After Manning dropped Colefield back at the cruiser, she sat and waited for a moment. Colefield rolled down the window. "What's up?"

She flashed him a sexy smile. "Catch me if you can..."

And then she sped off in a white dusty blur.

No way was Colefield going to play some foolish cat and mouse game, some rebound nonsense. He pulled out on to Front Avenue. He could just make out her jeep in the distance.

Then something broke in him. "Ah, the hell with it!" he said aloud, pushed the pedal to the metal and flipped on the siren and lights.

Despite his high-speed pursuit, he lost her, gave up and headed back to River Patrol Headquarters. When he pulled into the parking lot, Manning's jeep was sitting there, it's engine still hot.

Weaver was sitting at his desk, frumpish in his wrinkled uniform and untucked shirt.

"Where's Manning?" he asked.

Weaver pointed to the locker room. "What do you have going today?"

"Follow-up work mostly, why?"

"You're going to want to take the sled down to the Waterfront Pearl Towers ... it just came through the police scanner that a fire broke out there in the garage. Fire department responded and evacuated residents. One of the storage units burnt. They think it belongs to the girl found in the fountain last week."

"Where's the Lieutenant?"

"Personal day. He's moving his daughter into the dorms at U of O. She starts school there in the fall."

"Bart with the cadets?"

"No, Tony is. Bart made a run down to the shipyards."

"What's going on?"

"Threats of protests at Terminal 5 today."

"He went alone?"

"Someone needed to monitor the office."

"He shouldn't be by himself."

"Randal and Johnson from the Willamette office are meeting him there."

Manning popped out of the locker room wearing her uniform, tucking her hair up underneath her cap. "What's going on?"

"There's been a fire down at the Twin Towers. A storage unit."

"KK's?"

"Yep."

"Why'd I know that?"

It'd been quicker to drive the cruiser, but traffic had been a bear, even with the flashing lights and siren. The last fire truck was leaving the area as they pulled up and parked by the abandoned mounted patrol stables. Manning climbed out and ran off toward the bike path.

Colefield shouted: "Where're you going?"

"Give me a second!"

Colefield cleaned his sunglasses and then climbed out and sat on the hood of the cruiser and waited. She reappeared in a few minutes, jogging the short distance.

"The ship's still there. Let me make a call."

Manning pulled out her cell and spoke to someone named Petty Officer Green. Colefield didn't hear all the conversation but caught the drift of it.

"I informed the Coast Guard about the captain. They said, if the ship attempts to leave port, they'll detain it and call us."

"Nice work."

They switched gears and walked into the front lobby of the South Tower. Blake Brighton stood at the front desk and didn't smile when they entered. She had on a tan uniform, revealing traces of underarm perspiration.

Colefield did the talking. "What happened?"

Brighton swiped her sweaty brow with the back of her hand. "An hour ago, one of the residents pulled the fire alarm. The fire department said it looks like arson. I assume you're here because it's Ms. Kerns' unit?"

Colefield nodded.

Brighton reached under the counter and took out a large key ring. "We'll take the stairs; it's quicker."

She led the deputies down two flights of stairs to an underground parking structure. There were two levels, A and B. She told them that each tenant had a storage unit assigned to them as part of their purchase. The one assigned to Kris Kerns' unit had smoke damage on the exterior wall and yellow police tape strung across the door to block entry. The deadbolt had been broken out. Brighton said that the silver Mini Cooper parked off to the side was Ms. Kerns' vehicle. Though, it didn't show any signs of fire damage.

Colefield glanced inside the vehicle. She kept a clean car, just like she'd kept a clean-living space. The storage unit, on the other hand, was a mess.

The fire had destroyed everything. Flames had reached the ceiling but had not broken through the sheetrock. The few boxes that remained were soaking wet. The fire department had trashed the contents ensuring the fire was completely out. Nothing was smoldering that could reignite and further damage the building.

"Fire-retardant paint," Brighton explained. "The fire chief said it saved other units from catching fire."

"When did they leave?"

"Thirty minutes ago. They said it was probably arson."

"Where were you at the time?"

"At lunch."

"So, the front desk was unmanned when the alarm went off?"

"Yes."

Colefield thought to himself that if the intruder did their homework, they would have known this.

Manning walked over and tried to make out the contents of the burnt boxes. The fire had essentially destroyed everything. What was not ruined was so waterlogged that if you attempted to touch it, it would crumble. Manning pulled out a burnt client file and it fell apart in her hands.

Manning said. "We're not picking through this mess, are we?"

"Anything salvageable?"

Manning shook her head.

Colefield took a few photographs with his cell and then stepped out of the area.

"I have footage of someone running from the parking garage who the police believe may have started the fire. It's in my office, would you like to see it?" Brighton said.

Colefield stood there thinking. "How'd they get inside to set the fire?"

"The police think they used a key or picked the lock."

As they were leaving the parking structure, Colefield noticed several exits.

"Are cameras located in the stairwells?"

"No. Just battery-operated lighting in case of a fire."

They rode the elevator to the lobby and got off and followed Brighton to the front desk. There was a UPS guy just coming in the front door to drop off several packages that needed signatures. "Let me just put these in our mail room. Give me a moment."

Colefield snooped around the front desk while he waited. He fished through some memos from the HOA and other notices about upcoming maintenance repairs. There was a notepad with some doodling on it next to the phone. Colefield picked up the pad and thumbed through a few pages, examining the drawings, mostly harmless, mindless scribbling; until he came to the third page and noticed a stick figure drawing of a woman falling from a balcony. Colefield held it up and showed Manning.

He put the pad down just as Brighton reappeared.

"Follow me, deputies."

She led them inside a back office to the recording equipment. The monitor showed four active images of the building. The exterior, each lobby, and the underground parking structure.

Brighton said, "I need to reverse this slightly." She hit a button and studied the monitor.

The image on the bottom left flickered in fast motion. Brighton watched until it reached the right moment and pushed pause. "Here we are. Watch the garage door after the vehicle enters."

A car entered the parking garage but before the gate closed someone from the street entered.

"There…" Brighton pointed out. The intruder waited off in the shadows until the driver of the car parked and got into the elevator. They then moved in the direction of the storage units.

The intruder was slender and of average height. They wore loose-fitting sweatpants and a hooded sweatshirt that disguised their face. After removing a key from their pocket, they opened Kerns' storage unit and disappeared inside. A few minutes later, they came back out and left.

"Can you play it again?"

"Sure."

They all watched it a second time. Then Colefield asked: "Why isn't there smoke?"

Brighton fast-forwarded a few dozen frames. "There, see it now?"

A trail of smoke began to billow out. Colefield checked the time on the recording devise. Nearly ten minutes had gone by.

"I didn't see any accelerants being carried in. So, I wonder what they used..."

"The Fire Marshall said the fire started inside one of the boxes. He thinks it was chemically activated. He said he's seen that sort of thing in arson fires."

"No one was monitoring the footage?"

"We don't have the staff for that. It's only used if we have a situation in the building."

"And you showed this to the police?"

"Yes."

She reset the security system to live time and then stood up. "Unless there's something else, I need to return to the front desk."

Colefield hadn't paid much attention to it before, but he noticed that Brighton had strong B.O. It didn't fit her demeanor or tidy uniform.

Outside, after they had crossed the street, Colefield turned to Manning.

"Did you notice her B.O.?"

"You don't miss a thing, Colefield."

19

After speaking with Lieutenant Luis over the phone for the umpteenth time, they had to assume the captain had gone into hiding, but they weren't taking any chances. The Coast Guard assured them they would be alerted if the *Piranha* made a move during the night. Manning said she had a few more things to do around the office and she'd see him in the morning.

The sky was clear and cloudless with a deep reddish glow that was fading into the horizon. Streetlights were popping on along 82nd. Businesses advertising "XXX" were turning on their neon lighting. Several of the buildings advertised: "Live Models" and "Sex Shows".

Some habits were harder to kick than others. According to Montgomery, Susy Q Stanton was up to her old tricks again, working 82nd as a prostitute. Not the safest job, but she knew the territory and it probably paid well.

Manning's soon-to-be ex lived close by, so he figured he'd kill two birds with one stone. He hadn't told Manning what he was up to. He knew her well enough that she would have insisted on riding along.

Colefield figured the warm evening would attract customers, drawing men out of the shadows seeking ladies of the night. Unlike cities like Amsterdam or Berlin, prostitution in Portland was illegal. A john could be arrested, have their vehicle seized, and be thrown in jail. Colefield felt prostitution should be legalized and regulated just like Marijuana. It was the oldest occupation in the world; it wasn't going away anytime soon. But no one was asking his opinion.

The last picture he had of Susy Q was one he'd copied from her arrest records. He removed it from his t-shirt pocket and studied it. There were distinct features which probably hadn't changed from this early photograph. He was guessing that her pretty face would still be the same. As would her devilish cat-like eyes and long lashes. Overall, her body was pint-size except for breast implants which filled her out on top and added to her naughty appeal. The photograph showed her hair to be shoulder-length and dark. That he couldn't count on. She could have changed the color or length or preferred wearing a wig now. At the very least he could show her picture around to see if he could get any hits.

The first woman he saw standing under a streetlight had on fishnet stockings, platform heels, a mini skirt and see-thru blouse. He slowed his pickup and eased over to curb, rolling down his passenger window. The hooker walked over and peered inside.

"Hi honey, looking for something sweet tonight?"

Her face was too young and too round. Her eyes were green not ebony. Her hair was cut short and blonde. Colefield handed her the photograph along with a ten-dollar bill.

"I'm looking for someone special. Have you seen her around lately?"

The hooker frowned. She slipped the ten inside her bra and glanced at the photograph. "What you want her for when you can have me?"

"It's not personal. Just want to find her."

"Well, I haven't seen her. So long, honey. If you change your mind, I'm sure we could have some fun."

She stepped back from the pickup and strutted away.

He continued.

The next block had two girls working the same corner. He pulled off to the side and both sauntered over to his passenger window.

One was black, the other was white. They looked hardened and in their thirties. Both wore skimpy, see-thru tops and hot-pants. The black one did the talking. She leaned down and showed off her large breasts. "What ya in the mood for baby? A little black coffee and sugar?"

But before he could say anything, she either saw the photograph resting on the seat or read his intentions. "Never mind, baby — you don't look our type." She nodded toward her friend and they walked off. She must have figured he was a cop because they didn't want anything to do with him.

He circled the block and came back along the east side of 82nd. There were maybe a dozen women out working the sidewalks of a three-block area. It was a slow night and he only spotted two other cars pulling up to the curbs to proposition the hookers. One climbed into the front seat of a dark sedan and drove off. Another got into the back seat of a SUV, stayed a moment, and then climbed back out scowling at the driver before flipping him off.

He didn't see any police cars. They'd be working undercover, if they were out patrolling. He looked at all their faces as he slowly drove by and none of them resembled Suzy Q. He showed the photograph to two other hookers and neither of them knew anything. He was out thirty bucks and had turned up zip. Figuring it was time to give up, he decided to make one more sweep of the area and if he didn't see her, he'd call it a bust.

He passed a red neon porno shop sign and started to circle back when he saw a white Corvette slow down and pull over to the curb. A woman with long dark hair climbed out of the passenger door. She looked back and blew a kiss at the driver as he sped off. Colefield inched the pickup forward to get a closer look. Her face, hair color and eyes fit the bill. She had on cowboy boots, Daisy

Duke cut-offs that barely covered her crotch, and a skin-tight Harley-Davidson tank top that showed off her chest. He pulled over to the curb and stopped. She sauntered over to the passenger window and peered inside.

When she looked in at him, there was no mistaking it. Suzy Q had aged a little in jail, but it was her. He put his hand over the photograph before she saw it.

"Nice ride — want company?" she said, smiling in at him.

"Get in Suzy Q."

Her smile evaporated, knowing immediately he was not there for sexual favors. "Oh, shit — my lucky night. Let's get this over with…"

She climbed in, reached inside her small purse and pulled out a pack of cigarettes. "Got a light, cop?"

"Put 'em away."

She sighed. "What do you want?"

"Who was the guy in the Corvette?"

"A satisfied customer."

She looked over at him. He flashed his credentials.

"OK, Deputy, you shakin' me down?"

"It depends on how you answer the next few questions."

"Can I smoke or not?"

"Not."

She let out a heavy sigh again but put her cigarettes away, pouting. Colefield ignored her and drove down a side street for a few blocks until they came to a convenience store. He pulled into the parking lot and turned off the engine.

Under the bright streetlights, she looked rougher around the edges. Her nose was crooked, it had been broken and not reset properly. Her skin had red splotches. Her eyes were cold and filled with fight. She had two tiny scars on her right cheek.

"I understand you know Judge Elizabeth Brown?"

"She put me away that crazy cunt. I stay away from cunts."

"Are you certain of that?"

"What's going on here?"

"Where were you the morning of August 9th and the afternoon of August 11th?"

"Let me pull out my little black book and check."

"Don't be cute. I'm serious." She slunk back in the seat as if she was trying to distance herself and stared out the window.

"Simple question. Answer it or don't. Either way I figure you were involved."

"Involved in what?"

"Assaulting the judge."

"Have you lost your mind? I didn't assault anyone, especially not that bitch. She's nuts. I would never fuck with her."

She was a high-strung girl who needed to be smoking or drummin' her fingers over the seat constantly. She couldn't sit still.

"I'm waiting."

"The 9th and 11th? I met with my parole officer on Saturday morning. I can give you her number if you don't believe me."

"What about Monday afternoon?"

"When?"

"Between four and six."

She thought it over. "I was banging my boyfriend."

"And he'll corroborate that?"

"Damn better."

"Give me his phone number. If I find out you're lying, I'll be back. And one more thing —"

He pulled out the photographs of Peter Fink and Robby Hanson and tossed them on her lap. She picked Fink's photo up first.

"Who is this?"

"Thought you might have seen him around?"

"Nope."

"What about the other one?"

She tossed Fink's back and checked out the second image. "I might have seen this guy before. Real jerk. Likes to hit girls. I think my pimp took him for a ride recently. We haven't seen him back here since."

"Where did your pimp take him?"

"He never said."

"Did he kill 'em?"

"Has his body turned up?"

"Give me the name and number of your pimp."

"Can't do that. He'll cut me up if I give you that."

"Then were can I find him?"

"He hangs out at a Gentleman's club on Columbia near Martin Luther King when he's not hassling me. Look for a red Eldorado with a white interior. He's big, white and smokes fat cigars. You too should hit it right off."

She blew him a sarcastic kiss and left. He watched her strut inside the store and head toward the coolers in back. He picked up the matchbook she'd left behind on the seat. It had a phone number on it that he presumed was her alibi.

20

Richard lived alone now in the three-bedroom ranch-style house in southeast that he had once shared with Manning. The neighborhood seemed quiet, respectable. All the lights were off in the house when Colefield slowly drove by and circled the block before he parked a few houses down. He walked up to the front door and rang the doorbell and waited. After no one answered he went and checked the backyard. There was a six-foot fence surrounding the property. By the rear door was a food dish and water bowl but no dog. The yard was torn up. Roxy, bless her heart, was a digger. The lawn was a maze of craters and dirt piles, littered with steak bones and ratty baseballs.

Colefield had the basic layout of the property down in his mind and a rough plan worked out in advance. Returning to his truck, he kept an eye out for neighbors. He didn't see anyone peeking through their curtains. They probably had a good idea what Richard did for a living and figured it was best to steer clear of him.

Underneath the driver's seat, he kept a nightstick along with a roll of duct tape and a can of ether. The tape and ether were in a small bag that he could clip to his belt. He reached down and retrieved them. Stowed in the glovebox were a few canisters of mace and a spare .38 revolver. He wouldn't need Suzy Q's photograph any longer; her image was burned into his memory and would be for a very long time. He removed a canister of mace, placed it next to the nightstick but left the revolver. Then he put on a pair of leather gloves, grabbed the mace, nightstick, small bag and climbed out of his truck.

His greatest concern had been how to deal with the dog. A German shepherd would be a big dog to handle. Manning had told him to be cautious of Roxy. She could attack on command. He'd need to take precautions.

Colefield had been standing nearly an hour in the dark, rehearsing the plan over and over, trying to weed out the unknowns, when a pair of headlights turned into the driveway.

The car was a basic dark blue sedan with four doors. The type of vehicle issued to vice.

Richard Manning climbed out. He had on a loose-fitting Hawaiian shirt, slacks and loafers. Roxy was riding in back, sitting upright on the right side, sniffing out the window that had been cracked open to allow in air. The dog would probably smell him, but he'd worked this into his scenario. Depending on which side of the car he moved towards, he only needed a few seconds.

He hadn't counted on Richard to be holding a leash, which might prove to be a problem, but he had to go with it, take the risk.

As Richard walked around the front of the car and headed toward the rear passenger door, Colefield stepped out from the side of the garage and slipped up behind him. Richard must have sensed or heard trouble because he spun round like a street fighter, swinging the leash like a cord of rawhide.

Although he deflected it some, it still struck Colefield across the head and stung like a whip. But he kept his wits and sprayed the mace into the man's eyes and blinded him momentarily. It was just enough time to slip in and rap him alongside the temple with his nightstick. One swift, skilled, decisive hit was all it took to bring the big man tumbling to his knees, unconscious.

Roxy began barking. Her fangs looked menacing.

He had to hurry now.

Colefield removed the can of ether clipped to his belt, walked up to the rear window, and began spraying the ether into the car, doing his best not to hit the dog directly in the face. It took a few minutes before the powerful anesthetic took effect. Roxy stopped barking almost immediately and her growl was barely audible. Her front legs gave out and she collapsed onto the seat, conscious, but not able to move. She was breathing, smiling like a puppy.

Colefield checked his watch, the count began.

He pulled open the rear door. "Sorry about that Roxy."

He scooped her up and carried her toward his pickup.

21

Manning opened her apartment door with tears in her eyes. The effects of the ether were wearing off. Colefield needed to hurry. He spotted a sofa against the wall, carried the dog over and laid her down.

"What happened to her?"

"She'll be just fine in about..." He checked his watch. "In about five minutes. Be ready for anything."

She sat down next to the dog and kissed its nose.

"How'd Richard take it?"

"To the back of the head."

"You didn't..."

"I did. He'll need a few stitches, but he'll think twice about taking Roxy again."

Manning laughed with joy. "The bastard had it coming."

"Well, my work here is done." Colefield turned to leave.

"Where are you going?"

"Home. I need a shower and some sleep."

"Why don't you stay? I promise I won't jump your bones."

The thought of spending the night was tempting. But he had too many loose ends to tie up with Jill first. If he was launching off into a new romance, he wanted a clean break from the past. Right now, his heart wasn't ready.

"I'll take a raincheck."

"You're alright, Colefield. Bringing Roxy back was about the nicest thing anyone has ever done for me."

* * *

The following morning Colefield pounded on Montgomery's door, holding a cup of coffee in his free hand. He didn't hear anything inside, so he tried the knob. It was unlocked. He went inside.

The placed reeked of gun oil. "Bill! You around?"

He listened but didn't hear anything.

Instantly, a coldness washed over him. He sat his coffee mug down in the galley and headed for the spiral staircase.

The bedroom was its typical mess of war memorabilia: guns, knives, swords, endless magazines, newspapers, and scribbled-up yellow tablets. The morning newspaper lying on his unmade bed had not been opened. "Bill! You up here?"

More silence.

He checked the private bath nearby. The door was open, but it was unoccupied. He walked back across the room and noticed a light on at Montgomery's work bench at the back of the house. He went back to investigate.

Set up on a wooden bench, was a reloader, empty shells, and various gun cleaning supplies and parts. But no Montgomery...

He looked downstairs again and checked the back deck. He guessed the old pirate wasn't home and let out a sigh of relief. If he'd found him injured, or worse dead, it would have crushed him.

It was then that his cell phone rang. He reached in his rear pocket and pulled it out.

"Yeah!" he said.

"Is this Jason Colefield?" It was an older woman's voice but one that he didn't think he recognized.

"Who is this?"

"It's Jill's mother in New York."

"Mrs. Shapiro is everything alright?"

"Do you have a minute?"

Colefield picked up his coffee mug and took a sip.

"Go ahead."

"I'm not sure if I should be the one telling you this, but Jill left last night and hasn't come home."

The woman sounded as if she had been drinking. She was slurring her words.

"Mrs. Shapiro — Could she be visiting a friend?"

"What friends?"

"Are you OK, ma'am?"

She cut him off. "I'm just going to blurt it out. I lied. Jill has reunited with her high school sweetheart. That's where she was last night. Did you know that she came to New York for her high school reunion?"

"I thought she went to see you and her father."

"That's bullshit. She doesn't care about us."

"Ma'am you've been drinking. Will you please ask Jill to call me when she returns? I'd like to hear her side of this."

"Don't think you are going to win her back with your charm."

"Just give her the message."

Colefield hung up. He stood there staring down at the phone in his hand. He couldn't believe what he'd just heard, didn't know how much of it was a drunken ramble, or if any of it was true or not. He knew her mother had a drinking problem. But he didn't think it'd spill over into his life. But the longer he thought about it, he couldn't just let it go. He did a quick google search on his cell. He remembered where she had gone to school and entered it into the search bar. Sure enough, there had been a 15-year reunion held over the weekend. Maybe that explained Jill's erratic behavior lately.

This was not how he had expected his day to begin. He stuffed his phone back in his pocket staring down at Montgomery's kitchen table, replaying her mother's words over in his head, feeling both anger and pain. He almost missed the yellow tablet left in plain sight. Bold lettering across the top read: "COLEFIELD'S DIRTY TRIO." He picked up the tablet, skipped the part that mentioned Susy Q because he already had that information and went straight for the meat about the other two felons on the list. He read through the scribbles best he could and left with it.

Montgomery, once again, had delivered as promised. It was exactly the distraction he needed.

22

Manning was late. Colefield grew concerned that he couldn't reach her but needed to go.

Bart was checking his email on the computer. "You tried her cell?"

"I did," Colefield said. "Did she call in?"

"I've been here an hour. No calls."

Colefield paced. Bart turned toward him. He didn't want to go into details about Manning's dog. That was between them. And then there was the issue with Jill. He conjured up the worst, visualizing her rolling in the sack with her high-school sweetheart. He walked over and stared out the window. A flock of geese squawked by, but to Colefield it sounded like Jill crying out in pleasure.

"Tell Manning I couldn't wait any longer."

"Right-O. Back to Judge Brown's?"

Colefield nodded.

Grabbing his gear, he headed down to the boathouse. The fuel tanks on the sled were in good shape so he cinched his vest on and was about to shove off when Manning burst through the boathouse door with Roxy trotting behind. The dog spotted Colefield and growled.

"Roxy — knock it off!" Manning shouted. "Sorry I'm late. Roxy had a little incident on my carpet this morning..."

"I tried your cell. You have it turned off?"

She reached into her pocket. "Shit, yes. Sorry. Kind of rough start today. I couldn't leave her at the apartment. I don't trust Richard. For all I know he'd bust in, take her,

then have the locks changed to further spite me. Is it cool
with you if she hangs with us for a few days until I'm sure
it's safe to leave her alone?"

"You got a leash?"

Manning reached into her pocket, pulled a leather
strap out, and attached it to Roxy's collar.

"There's a special vest in the front compartment. You
might want to strap it on her."

"Bart said Judge Brown called again. What's up?"

"I don't know all the details, but they caught someone
on her roof this morning."

"Breaking in?"

"That's what were about to find out."

Manning shortened Roxy's leash and led her aboard.
Colefield didn't like the way the dog was glaring at him,
but he could hardly blame her, given the rough treatment
the night before. He kept his distance and focused on
firing up the engine. Diesel smoke filled the small
boathouse and Colefield backed the boat outside. The
fresh air felt good. He checked Manning, saw that she had
the vest on Roxy now and had secured her leash to her
seat. She turned and gave him the thumbs-up.

They were off. Colefield let off some steam as they
maneuvered upriver plotting a course to bypass Lemon
Island and head down the southern side of the channel,
keeping clear of the dolphins sticking up out of the
shallows.

At some point Manning removed her cap, shook out
her long dark hair, before tucking it back underneath her
cap. There was a calmness in her that hadn't been there the
day before. She turned and smiled. He caught a whiff of
her freshly washed body in the breeze and it aroused him.
She petted Roxy who seemed content staring off at the
wildlife along the shoreline.

For the briefest moment, Colefield almost felt happy.
The pressures on the job, his troubles with Jill, the
memory of the girl floating in the fountain, all vanished,

whitewashed from the slate. It was the closest he'd felt to being free-spirited in a long while.

The moment didn't last. The sled engines went quiet and the hull brushed along the narrow slip of the marina, jolting him out of his reverie.

Manning tied them off. "I think I'll leave Roxy aboard. She doesn't like cats."

Before they were even two feet from the boat, a drone buzzed overhead and Big Eddy waddled down the dock toward them, excitement filling his big eyes. He landed his drone at their feet.

"You made good time," he said and stared over at the German shepherd. "A patrol dog — how cool."

"Where's everyone?" Colefield asked, glancing toward Judge Brown's houseboat in the distance.

"We got it under control now."

"The Judge OK?"

"She's inside her place. Everything's groovy. Caught the boy red-handed trying to crawl through her upstairs window. Course he's denying it. Isn't that what little thieves do? Mendacious lot, all of 'em."

Manning said: "Tell us what happened."

"I can do better than that, I'll show you."

Eddy walked over and picked up his drone and charged off ahead.

Colefield was on guard and unfastened the strap on his Glock. He spotted a ladder alongside the judge's houseboat leading up to the roof. That troubled him. Manning noticed it too and glanced over at Colefield. She told Eddy to step aside and took the lead. She knocked hard on the Judge's front door.

The door opened. The Judge had on a gray suit, her hair was combed, she appeared calm.

"C'mon in," she said. "Let's get this over with."

Colefield hesitated, put his hand on his holster.

Eddy stayed put, allowing the officers to go in before he followed them inside and closed the door. Across the room, Fred and his nephew were sitting on a sofa a few feet apart, frowning. Neither of them looked like they wanted to be there. The nephew's eyes were darting around like he didn't want to make eye-contact with the deputies. Colefield secured his holster strap.

Judge Brown said: "What we have here is a little disagreement. Fred's nephew claims he was trying to help JC on my roof and was not trying to break in. Eddy caught it all on his drone camera. Looks to me like he was about to conduct a B & E while I was at work."

"Caught him red-handed," Eddy claimed. "Was about to bust-in her upstairs bathroom window."

"Now, Eddy, that simply isn't true," Fred said. "Ricky wouldn't do that. He told you what he was doing."

Judge Brown crossed her arms. "Then how do you explain the video? Eddy, show the recording to the deputies."

"This was taken from my drone this morning."

Manning squeezed in against Colefield's shoulder to get a better look at the small cell screen. Her body felt warm and hard.

The images that flashed before them showed Ricky climbing a ladder onto Judge Brown's upper deck, walking over and lifting the bathroom window open and then stepping back and looking around. Colefield assumed he'd heard the drone and got spooked.

Colefield looked over at the teenager. "What do you have to say?"

Ricky fidgeted around with his cell. His uncle snatched it away and put it down on the armrest of the sofa.

"I was trying to help her cat get back inside," Ricky said finally.

Eddy frowned. "Why would you do that?"

"Because JC was locked outside. She'd been meowing since Ms. Brown left for work. I wanted to help. Sometimes, the window accidently closes when she's outside. I wasn't going to break in. I've told you that. I just wanted to open it enough, so she could climb back in."

Colefield looked at the Judge. "Your call. His word against the video…"

The Judge rubbed the back of her neck, thinking. "Fred — you know your nephew better than any of us. Do you think he's telling the truth?"

Fred sat up straight. "Ricky is no thief. He's always been straight with me. I know he's been going through a rough patch, but I'd swear on a stack of Bibles, he's telling the truth."

"Ricky — why didn't you ask your uncle for help?"

"He was at the hardware store."

"Convenient time to break in," Eddy uttered.

"Eddy knock it off," Fred said. "You and that drone are driving us all crazy. Give it a rest."

"Nothing is missing, right?" Manning asked the Judge.

"No, it doesn't appear he came inside."

"The video confirms that," Colefield said.

Fred stood up. "Deputies, No harm, no foul, here. He was trying to do Elizabeth a favor and this is the thanks he gets? That poor animal would have been stuck up there all day in the hot sun with no water or food. And with all the hawks around, who knows what could have happened. Far as I'm concerned, my nephew is a hero."

Ricky reluctantly stood up, staying close to his uncle.

"Just a minute," Colefield said. "Judge, are you going to press charges?"

"I'm not completely sure who to believe. But JC was inside when I got home. If I have the boy to thank for that, so be it. If this sort of thing happens again, I would prefer he call me next time. It would prevent any air of misconduct."

Fred looked over at the Judge. "I'd like to look at your upstairs window. Perhaps it can be adjusted so this won't happen again."

"Go ahead, Fred. But leave Ricky here."

Fred shrugged and walked off. His heavy boots thudded up the spiral staircase.

Manning motioned for Eddy to join her outside. They left. Colefield waited for the Judge to speak.

"Hell, Jason," she whispered, "I thought he was committing larceny and he ends up rescuing JC." She turned toward Ricky. "I'm sorry. I haven't been myself lately. For a judge, this must look silly, making accusations and rash decisions. I appreciate what you did. You stay put for a moment; I want to give you something." The Judge walked into the kitchen and grabbed her wallet. She came back out and opened it, pulled out a twenty and held it out toward the teenager. "Take this. Do something for yourself. Let's put this behind us."

Ricky looked at the bill but didn't take it. "Ma'am, I don't need to be paid for what I did."

"I'd feel better if you took the money."

"Give it to my uncle if he fixes your window."

Ricky smiled weakly at Colefield and headed toward the door. Colefield nodded at the boy.

After he was gone, Colefield turned toward Judge Brown. "Any falls recently?"

"No. Thank god."

"Looks like he's telling the truth."

"I think he is. I feel like an idiot."

"He'll get over it, so will you. I've got some news about your list of felons. Ready for it now?"

The judge nodded.

"I located Suzy Q. She has alibis that checked out. I'm still working on locating the other two on the list."

"You'll let me know as soon as you find them?"

"Of course."

A few minutes later, Fred came back downstairs. He walked over to the Judge. "Window won't stay open, just as Ricky said. I'll grab my tools and fix it. Just needs a little adjustment."

The judge pushed the twenty into his hand. "Ricky wouldn't take it."

Fred looked down at the money. "Doesn't seem right." He handed the bill back. "We got to look out for each other."

Outside Colefield saw Manning speaking with Ricky over at the sled. She had untied Roxy and was letting the boy pet the dog. The boy and the dog hit it off.

When Colefield walked up Roxy growled.

23

Feinstein called as they were taking the sled back to the shed. Colefield talked to him for a few minutes and then put his cell away.

"We have another body," Colefield said. "Roxy need to take a leak or anything?"

"She's good. Who is it?"

"A jogger found a body in some bushes north of the Broadway Bridge. It's a male, mid-to-late thirties, Hispanic, they think. That's all they got so far. Feinstein's going to meet us there. It's a couple hundred yards down river from the Twin Towers."

"He wouldn't be calling us unless he thought it had a connection to the girl in the fountain."

"Those were my thoughts."

"Something happen to you recently?" Manning asked. "You seem different today?"

"I may have to dump my girlfriend."

He had a serious expression now. Manning noticed it. "Think it's a wise decision?"

"Too early to tell."

* * *

As they motored by the Twin Towers, he flashbacked to the girl in the fountain. He saw her floating there, kimono open, blood oozing out in a starburst over the water. How little they still knew about her. Now another body, so close to where they had found hers, it didn't seem like just a coincidence.

The dead man was stocky, dark-skinned — not African America — probably Spanish or Hispanic. His body was face down in a bed of green shrubbery. There was congealed blood at the back of his head as if he'd been struck several times from behind with a blunt object. He had on black slacks and a blood-stained white shirt.

A small crowd gathered near the patch of rhododendron a few yards from the bike path. The area was sectioned off with crime scene tape and a few uniforms were keeping the public back. An ambulance crew and some paramedics from the fire department were on scene. News crews were busy setting up cameras. The parade was in full swing ... a similar scene taken from the dead girl's playbook.

Feinstein's cruiser pulled off the main road and followed a service road down to where the others lingered. When the detective got out, Colefield spotted him and nodded. They met up at the scene. Neither of them said anything.

Manning stayed behind for a few minutes securing Roxy before she eventually pushed her way to the front. "Hello to you to, Bev." Feinstein said, pulling out his notebook.

Manning ignored the comment, got within a few feet of the body, and turned back toward them. "Colefield! Come over here."

Colefield moved in closer.

One of the lab techs was told to roll the body over. Manning was not one to show emotion, but the stench of the decaying corpse was very pungent. Once it was jarred it released air trapped deep within its core and the odor was gagging. She stepped back, covering her mouth and nose. "It's our missing captain," she said, losing the hard edge to her voice, trying not to puke. "Smells like he's been dead awhile."

"That explains why he's been hard to locate." Colefield studied the area before he moved back.

Feinstein made a few notes then walked over. "What'd you say?"

Manning said: "The victim — he was the captain aboard the *Piranha*."

"Well, that's just great. There goes our number one suspect."

Manning looked over at one of the officers. "Did you find a wallet or cash on him?"

"We haven't searched the body yet, ma'am. Waiting on the M.E."

Manning looked over at Feinstein. "There's a reason he was near the towers ... don't you think?"

Feinstein put his notebook away. "Why don't you and Colefield head back to the ship and see what you can find out?"

Manning took another look at the body before moving further back. Someone from the crowd stepped up to her from behind. Colefield caught a glimpse of the man as Manning spun round, edgy, her guard up. Colefield tensed-up and moved in closer to her.

"What the hell are you doing here?" Manning snapped. It was Richard again. Different suit. A green one today. But he still had his gold shield displayed on his belt. He had a few new scratches on his face. His eyes had bags under them. Colefield liked that he looked like hell.

"I'm on the job. Got a problem with that?"

Manning's voice cracked. "You're stalking me, damnit!"

"Don't flatter yourself."

Richard turned and cocked his finger at Colefield and pulled an imaginary trigger. He smirked and walked over to Feinstein. "What happened here?" he asked the detective. Feinstein remained professional, but Colefield could tell he didn't like the guy.

"Who called vice?" Feinstein asked.

"I was in the area, heard it on the radio. Thought it might be one of my douche-bags."

It sounded like a lie.

"We've got this..." Feinstein said.

Richard glanced at the body. "Not the guy I'm looking for," he said, and walked off.

He stopped and turned toward Manning: "See you around, Bev honey ... you too, Colefield! And I'll be seeing Roxy soon. Guaranteed..."

After he was gone, Feinstein walked over.

"He's dangerous," Colefield said.

They both looked over at Manning, biting down on her lip, like it was all she could do not to pull out her Glock and shoot the bastard in the back of the head.

"Get her out of here before she blows a fuse. See what you can find out across the river."

Colefield nodded. He stepped back and bumped into a female jogger, who had stopped to check out the excitement. It took him a moment to recognize her.

"Ms. Brighton, what are you doing here? This is police business."

"Since when is it illegal to get in a little exercise before I start work?"

Colefield noticed that she wasn't the least bit sweaty. A carrying case was strapped to her right leg, longer and narrower than a cell phone holder and too round for a bowie knife.

She glanced over at the body, her face showing no emotion. "I recognize the guy. He's been at the towers a few times."

"Is that right?"

"What happened to him?"

"I can't discuss anything with you."

"Why deputy, I sense that you don't like me very much."

"I've been known to rub people the wrong way. What's that thing strapped to your leg?"

"It deters the pervs along Waterfront Park."
And with that, Brighton jogged off toward the towers.

24

After they boarded The *Piranha*, Lieutenant Luis came out on deck. He hadn't shaved, his eyes were bloodshot, his uniform wrinkled.

"Officers, have you located our captain?"

Manning looked at Colefield. He figured it was his turn to break the bad news, but this didn't seem like the appropriate place. "Is there somewhere inside we can speak in private?"

"Yes, of course, follow me."

They moved inside the ship to the galley. There was a small sitting area with picnic style benches. The door to the kitchen was ajar. They sat down at the table.

Colefield cleared his throat. "I'm sorry about this — but your captain was found dead this morning. His body was discovered across the river along the riverbank in some bushes. We are treating it as a homicide."

Luis swallowed hard, staring at Colefield with hollow eyes.

Manning tucked a few loose strands of hair up under her cap. "Did he ever show up after he left last Saturday?"

"No, I would have notified you."

"What about Felipe? Has he told you anything more?"

"He blames himself for our predicament. He says it was not the captain that pushed her."

"Then who?"

"With Felipe, nothing is certain. But I believe the captain was there that night. He may have been on the balcony but there was someone else involved."

"We'll need to speak with him again."

"Felipe is still very ill. And once he learns of the captain's death, I fear he will have a stroke. Do you have any suspects?"

"Does Felipe believe it's possible the killer saw him that night from the balcony?"

"It is possible. But he has not said this for certain. Why would somebody kill our captain?"

"Perhaps he was murdered because of his connection to Ms. Kerns' death that night. It's possible he saw who pushed her off the balcony and he was killed because of it."

Manning added: "And Felipe may be in danger now. When the captain returned to the ship Friday night, what did he do?"

"He went to his cabin and changed uniforms."

"Why?"

"I don't know. But he showed up at the bridge shortly thereafter wearing a freshly pressed uniform. He relieved me for a spell, and then he left the ship again early the following morning as I've said."

"Is that uniform here?"

"It should be..."

"We'll need to see his quarters."

"Of course."

Manning said to Colefield: "He may have been destroying evidence..."

"No," Luis cut in, eyeing her coldly. "He is an honorable man. He did not kill anyone."

"Someone did."

"And we have been cooperating, but you must understand the devastation of this latest news. I think it would be best to refrain from telling Felipe. I will break it to him as soon as he is stronger."

Colefield glanced at Manning and nodded. "Fair enough."

As they left the galley, Colefield noticed the kitchen door had closed.

The small living quarter was tidy. There was a writing desk against one wall and a small dresser drawer next to it. On the other side were two small closets and a single bed near a tiny port window that looked toward the west side of the river. Manning walked over and looked out, turned back, and nodded to Colefield.

Nothing was out of place except for an antique spyglass lying on the end of the bed, as if someone had used it recently.

Manning walked over to the closet and opened it. Hanging inside was one dress uniform and four daily wear summer uniforms, pressed, along with some polished shoes. She pulled out the uniforms, one at a time, and looked them over before moving on to the second closet that held cold weather gear, a life jacket, headgear and rubber boots.

"Nothing here."

"Check the dresser."

The lieutenant was closer, so he pulled open each drawer, revealing well-organized drawers of white and black t-shirts, jockey shorts, jeans, and various wool and lightweight socks.

"No one came in and cleaned his uniforms?"

"No, ma'am."

"How many dress uniforms are standard issue?"

"Officers are allowed one. The crew is not issued dress uniforms."

"Who is responsible for cleaning them?"

"We send them out. We have two washers and dryers aboard but no way to steam press."

"Did the captain send his uniforms out for cleaning on Friday?"

"I don't think so."

"Where does the crew store dirty laundry?"

"We have a laundry drop."

"Show us."

The laundry room was being used when they entered. Two crew members were folding clothes on a narrow table across the room. Both washers and dryers were running. Some smelly clothing was thrown into a laundry box in the corner. Colefield walked over to it.

"Are undergarments marked?"

"Yes, with initials of the crew member."

Colefield looked at Manning. "Got any gloves with you?"

"Fresh out."

"Great."

Colefield reached down into the dirty clothing and pulled out a pair of soiled underwear. He read the markings on the tag, tossed it aside and dug down deeper, removing a second pair of jockey shorts. He checked the tag. It had the correct initials.

"Bingo."

He held them up to the light. There were stains in the front, what looked like semen.

He placed them on the table beside the two crew who were watching. "I'll need something to put these in. A Ziploc would be preferable."

"I'll get one from the galley," Luis said. "I'll be right back."

Luis left, followed by the crew with their laundry baskets. Colefield glanced at the dirty shorts, thinking. "A jealous lover..." he said. "There was someone else in the condo that night. I believe Ms. Kerns was having sex with more than just the captain and someone walked in on them..."

25

The sick bay was located at the back of the stern. The door with the red cross was closed when they reached it. Lieutenant Luis opened it, glanced inside, then turned and faced the deputies, looking surprised.

"He's gone."

"Let's go check his bunk." Colefield said, holding the Ziploc bag at his side.

It was a short hike down another flight of stairs to the crew's quarters. The area had a familiar cramped and lonely feel, Colefield thought. Felipe's bunk was on the end, a lower bunk, with poor lighting. The bed had been slept in recently.

"Maybe he's went to use the head," The Lieutenant said. "Wait here, I'll check."

Colefield sat down on one of the bunks and slipped back in time, remembering his last days in the Navy. There were rumors then that their cutter was going to be sent to South America to wage war on drug trafficking, and his enlistment was going to be extended by a year — not by choice. His last memory was packing his duffel bag with his few belongings on a bunk no larger than the one he was sitting on now, wondering what lie ahead.

Manning checked her watch. "What's taking Luis so long?"

Colefield snapped out of the reverie and stood up. "Give him a minute more."

"I don't like it."

"Like what?"

"Doesn't feel right."

"Where would he go?"

"I'm not talking about the Lieutenant. I'm talking about Felipe."

Manning took off down the narrow corridor. Colefield sighed and took off after her.

They eventually found the head. Colefield stepped around Manning and went inside. He came out shaking his head.

"I told you," Manning said.

"Maybe the Lieutenant took him back to sick bay."

"That's not my first thought."

It was then that they heard a dog begin to bark outside the ship.

"It's Roxy!" Manning hustled toward the nearest exit. Colefield was right behind her.

The bright sunlight struck him hard. Colefield put on sunglasses and looked around. Then he saw the Lieutenant peering down over the side, shouting at someone below in the water.

Lieutenant Luis spun round. "He has jumped overboard!"

"Felipe?"

"Yes, yes!"

The deputies peered over the stern toward the water. A small lifeboat with two Hispanic crew members aboard paddled fiercely toward a body floating in the river, 20-feet ahead of them.

"He must have been in the kitchen and heard us talking about the captain! Didn't I warn you he would take the news hard!"

"We'll get him!" Manning said.

The deputies returned to their boat in a hurry. Manning got ahold of Roxy's leash and held her firmly while Colefield took the helm. The lifeboat was in the near distance, the crew struggling to pull Felipe's limp body out of the river. Even from where Colefield was he could tell the crew had been too late.

By 6 pm, the sun was a scorcher. Too warm even for the seagulls who sat ashore in the shade but not the Jet skiers blasting by, unaware of the drowning.

Manning swiped her sweaty brow, tired, spent, still visibly shaken by the death of the old cook. After they finished with the Lieutenant aboard, she climbed down from the *Piranha* into their boat. She got ahold of Roxy's leash and motioned that it was safe for Colefield to begin the descent.

After he dropped down from the rope ladder, the boat rocked from side to side and threw him off balance. He got ahold of the steering wheel and waited until the river quieted down some. Then he told Manning to untie the lines from the *Piranha*. Hopefully, for the last time.

"What a fucked-up day," Manning mumbled, as she shoved off, and got ahold of Roxy again. "I've been thinking," she added later, "about what you said. If there was another lover involved — then, why isn't there footage of them in the lobby?"

"Maybe there was, and we missed it."

Colefield pulled out the Ziploc and tossed it to Manning.

"Stow this in an evidence case."

She caught it seconds before Roxy did and stowed it in a Pelican Case from the storage hold.

"Who do you think we missed? Not the guy in the black cap?"

"No Feinstein cleared him. Someone else… What we know for certain was that the video had confirmed the captain arrived at Ms. Kerns' last. Ample time for him to run into the killer."

"Then why didn't he mention it to us when we interviewed him the first day?"

"Maybe he felt responsible for her death. It doesn't add up, unless it was an accident."

"And it got him killed later..."

"My thought exactly. It's not common for a killer to revisit the crime scene," Colefield said.

"You think he left something behind?"

"Or — someone wanted revenge and lured him back."

Manning thought it over. "Or, the concierge is lying."

"We both know the parking structure and the lobbies were under surveillance. She could have known that and found a way around the cameras."

"I'm liking the way you're going with this..."

Manning checked her watch. "She's still on shift, right?"

"Let's go find out."

26

The fresh scent of lemon oil reminded him of something that he couldn't place. Colefield stepped back from the front desk while the male concierge finished polishing the countertop.

The concierge ignored them for a moment while he finished. He put the aerosol down and pulled a box of Kleenex out from under the counter and set it next to a small vase with a single yellow daffodil.

"How can I help you?"

Colefield glanced around. "We're looking for Ms. Brighton. Is she here?"

"I'm afraid not."

"Where is she?" Manning asked.

"She quit. I was called in to fill her shift."

Colefield glanced toward the back room as if he didn't believe it. "You're sure about that?"

"Not only sure, I'm pissed. It's my day off. I had plans."

"We'll need her home address."

"Give me a moment."

The attendant disappeared into the back room. Colefield could hear filing cabinets opening and closing. A few minutes later, the young man returned empty-handed.

"That's kind of strange..." he uttered.

"What?"

"Her personnel file is gone."

"Gone?"

"Gone."

"Who took it?

"Good question."

"Did she take it with her?"

"How would I know? She wasn't here when I arrived."

Manning turned to Colefield and shrugged.

"How long has she worked here?"

"Two or three months."

"Is there a vetting process?"

"No. We submit a resume and wait to hear back?"

"What about a background check?"

"I'm sure the company does that."

"Do you ever get to see the results?"

"We either get the job or we don't."

"Brighton attend college?"

"You're asking me all these things that I don't know."

"I think you do."

"OK — so maybe we chatted between shifts. We both graduated from PSU. I have a degree in business management. Hers is psychology."

Manning said: "I'll need to check the backroom myself."

Colefield figured Manning could handle it. While she went and checked there, he kept his eye on the concierge, resting his elbow on the counter.

"Was Ms. Brighton a good employee?" he asked, aware he was smudging the polished desk.

"She did her job."

"You didn't like her very much?"

"No."

"Why?"

"She had issues."

"Go on..."

"She was a little too friendly with the residents. It was becoming a problem. It's good she quit."

"Anyone in particular?" Colefield asked.

"Ms. Kerns for one."

"You're sure about that?"

"A few weeks back, I saw her leave her condo with lipstick on her cheek. Doesn't take a genius to figure out what she was doing. She tried wiping it off before I could notice."

"This information would have been helpful to the police."

"No one asked me."

"Who else was she sleeping with?"

"I don't know, she was secretive."

Manning returned. She looked at them both. "Her file is gone."

Colefield was staring at the clerk, thinking about what he'd said.

They left the building and stopped along the sidewalk outside. "I'm going to call Feinstein," Colefield said.

"What were you and the clerk talking about?"

"He thinks Brighton was having an affair with Kerns. Maybe others in the building, too."

"Kerns?"

Colefield nodded. "Call DMV, see if you can get a home address for her."

Manning checked her watch. "Shit, where'd this day go. It's after 6, they're closed."

Colefield and Feinstein talked for a few minutes, and then Colefield hung up and put his cell away.

Manning was growing impatient. "Well?"

"He's going to try and get an address. He'll be in touch."

27

When they got back to the shed, the place was dark. They went inside and turned the lights on. Manning found a dish by the sink and carried some water out to Roxy while Colefield filled out a chain-of-custody for the evidence he had collected from the ship. He took the sample and the form and placed it on Bart's desk with instructions to drop if off at the lab downtown. Next, he sorted through mail in his inbox.

They both caught up on paperwork, answered emails, and then after an hour, they looked over at each other and agreed to call it a day.

Colefield changed out of his uniform into blue jeans and a t-shirt and was tying his shoe when Manning walked in to the dressing room.

He looked over at her. "What's up?"

Manning was combing out her long hair, staring at him. She had changed into shorts and a tank top, had put on some makeup, which made her dark eyes stand out. There was something behind those amber-colored eyes that Colefield couldn't read.

"Heard from your girlfriend yet?" she asked casually.

"Matter of fact, no."

"What are your plans tonight? I don't especially feel like going home to an empty house."

"Want to get a drink? I could use one."

"You twisted my arm."

They drove across the river and parked on the Washington side, down from the Interstate Bridge, a small park, with plenty of oaks, and a narrow beach were Roxy could go for a run. There were a few other cars in the lot. But no people around. After they walked over to the restaurant and got drinks in plastic cups, Manning let Roxy loose.

"I'm going to grab a blanket from my car. Keep an eye on Roxy, would you? I'll catch up with you."

Colefield followed a path down to the river. He knew the area well. The river was shallow along the shoreline, no steep drops. It was a good place to catch the sunset. He let Roxy go for it, watched her splash around in the water and sat down on a log. It was a sandy area, so he set his drink aside, kicked off his shoes, felt the cool sand on the bottom of his feet.

A few minutes later, Manning appeared, handed Colefield her drink while she laid out a blanket on the sand. She glanced over toward the water where Roxy was playing. There were a few other people down the beach, but no one nearby. They had the area to themselves — their own private oasis away from the craziness of the city.

Manning kicked off her shoes, took her drink back, and sat down on the blanket, relaxed back against the log.

"It's nice down her tonight." She said.

"This was a good idea. I needed to unwind. It was a hell of a day."

"And I thought all River Patrol did was float around and look at nude sunbathers."

"It's not always like today."

"You're just trying to cheer me up."

"Speaking of that, any more problems with the Ex-to-be?"

"I hired a hot-shot lawyer. He's pissed as hell. But let's not talk about him. It's too nice of a night to spoil it."

"It'll blow-over in time."

"Maybe ... or I'll just have to shoot him." She smiled.

Colefield sat down on the blanket beside her, their shoulders touched. They drank and watched Roxy frolic along the river's edge, chasing a few seagulls. Manning got up and threw her a stick, which she fetched. They did that for a while until Roxy plopped down in the sand nearby and began chewing on the stick, content for the moment.

The sun began setting, casting a warm orange glow over the water. The air smelled fresh and clean; there was a light breeze, which made it just right. In the distance the Interstate Bridge slowly fell into shadow and the headlights of passing cars generated little distant halos against the sky.

It was a perfect night...

It just sort of came out unexpectedly...

He leaned over and kissed Manning on the lips. She pulled back slightly, gave him a mixed message, a "what-the-fuck-look", and just when he thought he'd been out of line, she put her hands on his shoulders, pushed him down on the blanket and rolled on top, taking control. She smiled down at him. Then she planted her warm lips on his.

For a while, they kissed like teenagers. And then Manning sat up, peeled off her top and bra and tossed them aside. *Smitten...*

28

The night had been too special to let it go — a mirage of impressions, feeling and sensations, rippling through his body. Colefield couldn't sleep. He got up before his alarm sounded and went into the galley to make some coffee. He couldn't remember the last time he felt something special…

This was day nine. Ms. Kerns had been dead over a week and they were only just now skimming the surface of her life. In that time, he'd witnessed a drowning, seen death so close it felt personal, and had a new partner, turning his world inside out.

Even Calico Jack recognized the change. She sat on the windowsill, watching him move about with renewed vigor.

His walk was more deliberate, his eyes no longer forlorn. There was a hint of a smile and if you listened closely, humming spilled from his lips as he filled the coffee pot and while he opened a can of cat food. Calico Jack liked the new him. She jumped down on the floor and rubbed up against his leg, purring.

Shit, what was he thinking? This feeling couldn't last — he was just fooling himself, like he had so many times before…

Just as his thoughts darkened, his cell rang in the other room. He thought of just letting it ring. If it was Jill, she would sense immediately he'd cheated on her. If it was Feinstein, then he knew he'd have more work to do and he needed a little time to himself.

Just let the bastard ring…

But he couldn't.

It was neither of them, nor was it First Alert, which was a relief. And, it wasn't Manning either. It was the last person he expected.

"Elizabeth," he said. "Everything all right?"

"Sorry to call so early, Jason. I couldn't sleep last night. I kept thinking about Kris Kerns and that list of felons I gave you. Have you made any progress tracking down the killer or those scumbags?"

He'd almost forgotten what he'd promised. "I'm sorry, Elizabeth. I was meaning to call. We're slowly getting a picture of what might have happened to your friend. I should have more to go on later. I'm waiting for Detective Feinstein to get back to me."

"Sorry to be a pest. What about the list?"

"I've narrowed it down to one. The other two weren't around. One was in jail in Astoria, the other was with her P.O. or pimp or boyfriend, I can't remember which now. I have Fink's address. I'm going there today. Right after I hang up."

"You think Peter Fink is the guy?"

"I don't know. I need face time with him."

"Well, if he's responsible...cut him a new asshole."

Before he could comment, the line went dead. The judge always got right to the point.

After coffee, he called Feinstein to see what the hold up was on the address he needed. An hour later, he was meeting both Manning and Feinstein for breakfast at the Dockside. It hadn't been his or Manning's choice, it was Feinstein's. He had the information they wanted but was holding it hostage until they bought him breakfast. He told them, after they sat down at a booth, that if he didn't have a real meal soon, he might shrivel up and die.

"The wife is going to kill me with this diet. If I don't eat a little bacon and white toast soon, I'll shoot myself," were his very words.

"Why don't you give up the diet. It doesn't sound like it's working for you."

"And then what? I hate cooking. My wife will divorce me. Man cannot live on hotdogs alone."

Manning looked down at his belly. "You could lose 10-pounds, but I wouldn't sweat it."

Feinstein was still harping about the diet when the waitress arrived at the table with coffee and menus.

"Just tell your wife you're too old to change."

Manning rearranged her silverware and laughed. She opened her menu. "I'm hungry. This was a great idea. Feinstein, if you want a large order of biscuits and gravy, I say go for it."

"Thank you, Manning. At least someone around here has a heart."

Colefield held back a smile. "So how long are you going to hold out?"

"It's been a week."

"I meant with the address."

"Give it a rest. You haven't paid the bill yet."

The waitress arrived to take their order. Colefield was curious what Feinstein would have and passed on coffee. He'd already had enough caffeine in his system that he felt his hands were rattling. He ordered a milkshake instead.

"You're doing that to spite me," Feinstein pointed out.

The waitress waited patiently. "Need more time here?"

Feinstein couldn't make up his mind. "You two go ahead."

Manning ordered a half-order of eggs benedict. In addition to his milkshake, Colefield ordered corn beef hash, eggs over-easy. And, homemade tortillas on the side.

Feinstein was sweating over what to order. "Ah, shit — bring me some oatmeal with blueberries."

Colefield smiled over at Manning. He said to the waitress as she started to walk off. "You might want to check back in a few minutes. The detective may want to change his order."

She walked off, shaking her head.

Feinstein felt his pocket for his cigarettes. He knew he couldn't smoke inside, but he needed reassurance that some things wouldn't change. He eventually gave in and pulled out a piece of paper, tossed it down in front of Colefield.

"I can arrange for a black & white if you need backup," he said.

"We're just going to talk with her. As far as we know, she hasn't committed a crime."

"Well, you're not going to like who she's living with."

"Why do you say that?"

"Remember the run-in you had down at Terminal 6 with one of the union guys?"

"She lives with him? Great. I'll see if I can avoid his right hook."

Manning sipped her coffee and then told Colefield she needed to use the head. He stood up and let her out of the booth. She winked at him. "Colefield's a tough guy, he can handle anyone."

After she was gone, Feinstein stared at him.

"What?" Colefield said.

"I see how the two of you are looking at each other."

Colefield turned serious. "What the hell am I going to tell Jill?"

"That's up to you, buddy boy. It's not her I'd be worried about. I'd be careful around Manning's Ex. He might not like the idea that you're banging his wife."

Manning rejoined them. When Colefield slid in beside her, Manning squeezed his inner thigh affectionately. He felt her sensual heat radiating and gulped down his milkshake to put out the fire.

Breakfast was served. Manning carved her meal into little pieces and ate slowly. Colefield noticed Feinstein was picking at his oatmeal, not really wanting it.

"Want a tortilla?" Colefield teased.

Feinstein put his spoon down and flagged down the waitress, who came back over to the table. "Everything all right?"

He slid his uneaten oatmeal toward her. "Bring me a stack of pancakes, a side of bacon, and three eggs over easy."

"Want hash browns?"

"Sure, throw some of those in. And bring me some toast. The whiter the better. And plenty of butter and maple syrup."

Feinstein relaxed. He sipped his coffee and just stared at the two deputies. "Something on your mind?"

"Good for you," Colefield said. "Life's too short for dieting."

"You're still buying..."

"A deal is a deal."

After breakfast, Feinstein could barely climb out of the booth. He loosened his belt one notch but had a smile from ear to ear.

"Great idea coming here," he said on the way out.

Feinstein waddled out to his dark sedan and climbed in behind the wheel. Colefield's truck was parked down the street near Manning's jeep. He walked Manning to her car. The windows were part way down, and he could see Roxy sitting in the passenger seat, eyeing some small birds.

Manning got in and rolled down her window. Roxy glared over at him.

"You still good about last night?" he asked.

"More than good. You?"

"Couldn't be better..."

29

The Lighthouse was a fleabag motel off Burnside and Stark, near the Spartacus Sex Shop. The building was slated for demo soon. On the drive over, Colefield had called the front desk to verify Fink was still living there.

The clerk running the front desk was a chain-smoker, a nervous looking guy. He had on a checkered short-sleeve shirt, which showed off an anchor tattoo on one arm and a panther on the other.

Colefield walked up to the desk and flashed his credentials. "I called earlier about Peter Fink."

His fingers, stained from years of nicotine, lifted off the counter. "He's in room 301. Take the stairs in back." He pointed where to go.

"Anyone with him?"

"Better not be."

"Any trouble?"

"Nah — he's as quiet as a hummingbird."

Colefield took the stairs in back. The building was on its last days all right. The woodwork was peeling, faded, chipped. The stairs squeaked and felt unsteady. The carpet in the hall was stained and smelled like dirty socks. Bulbs were burnt out everywhere. The place was dark, its own kind of hell. That said, it beat sleeping on the street.

Colefield knocked on the door of room 301. He could hear a radio playing inside. He heard a heavy clunky sound moving toward the door before he heard the chain lock come off and scrape across the wood. The door opened.

The young man was shirtless, needed a shave, hair a greasy mess. He wore baggy jeans with no belt. His B.O. made the deputy's eyes water. "Yeah?" he said, leaning his weight on his left crutch. "What do you want?"

"You Peter Fink?"

"Who's asking?"

"May I come in?"

"Not until you tell me what this is about."

"Has to do with Judge Brown."

"Oh, shit ... don't trip over anything."

The single room was small and cluttered with old paperbacks, clothing, dirty dishes, and porno magazines. There was a hotplate and a single bed and dresser. One chair and a worn sofa. It was cramped for one, but squeezing two in, made it even more claustrophobic.

"I got to get off this leg," he said. "It's killing me."

"What happened?"

"Some knucklehead ran me down on a bicycle. Doctor said he broke the femur in two places. They had to put a steel rod in. Might never get full use of it again."

The guy flopped down on the sofa. He set his crutch aside.

"How long you been laid up?"

"Ever since I got out of jail. Happened the same day. I got all the luck."

"What was the date of the accident?"

"You ask a lot of questions, Mr."

"It's Deputy Colefield."

"Whatever. What do you want? Judge Brown have it in for me again?"

"I was going to ask you the same thing."

"What are you talking about?"

"When did you get out of jail?"

He glanced toward a calendar hanging on the wall. I can't see it from here. Go over and look at the date circled in red."

Colefield complied.

The month was August. The date circled was the 3rd.

"You're certain that is the day?"

"You see any other days circled?"

"It's not you," he said aloud, putting it together in his head. "The time frame doesn't match."

"Don't know what you're talking 'bout, bub. What's the judge accusing me of now?"

"Breaking into her place and assaulting her."

"She put me away nearly three years the last time. I wouldn't go near her. Whatever she said I did, I didn't. How could I with this bum leg?"

"Point taken. You ought to get someone in here to clean up. You don't want to fall and break the other leg…"

30

Later that afternoon they grabbed a cruiser and headed over to Washington to the address Feinstein had given them. The modern yellow house sat on a hill a few miles east of downtown Vancouver with a daylight basement and a view of the Columbia River. There was a detached two-car garage with a Ford pickup parked in front, and RV parking along the side. The RV lean-to sat empty.

Manning glanced over at Colefield. "Feinstein better be right," she said.

Colefield punched in the Ford's license plate. "Truck is registered to a Frank Brighton. I see here he also owns a 2010 Lincoln, two ATV's, and a 2013 Thor Outlaw Motor Coach."

"What about the girl?"

"I'm showing nothing registered in her name with DMV."

"Maybe daddy lets her drive his Lincoln."

"Let's go ask him."

They climbed out of the cruiser and hiked up a path of stairs to the front door and rang the bell, one of those electronic surveillance doorbells, alerting the owner in advance who's on their porch.

After a few moments the door opened. Frank Brighton didn't seem surprised to see them.

"She's not here," he said in a deflated voice.

"Do you know where she is?"

Brighton smelled like alcohol. "Why don't you come in and we can discuss it."

The deputies were a little apprehensive but followed Frank Brighton back inside and closed the door. They performed a quick survey of the rustic interior and then entered the living room. It had comfortable over-stuffed sofas and recliners, long drapes and large windows and walls decorated with antlers. In back, sharp-shooter trophies sat inside a walnut showcase.

"Nice trophies…" Manning said to break the ice.

"Some of those are Blake's. She shot her first six-point when she was thirteen. She tagged a bear when she was fifteen. She's a hell of shot with a 30-06."

"Does she have a gun with her now?"

"I don't know."

"Is there anyone else in the house?"

"No. It's just the two of us who live here."

"Where's her mother?"

"She died when she was twelve. Can I get either of you something to drink?"

"No thanks," Colefield said. "We came for Blake."

"I got a few things to tell you first. Have a seat. I'm going to refill my glass."

Frank Brighton disappeared into the kitchen and returned with a rocks glass of Bushmills. He motioned for them to sit. He slid into a recliner and took a sip of his drink.

"She left this morning," he said, as if the thought of it still stung. "She left in the motorhome. I don't know if she's coming back…"

"Why's that?" Colefield said.

"It's just felt like she was running away."

"What makes you think that?"

"Blake has always been different. From a child on…" The man took another glug of his drink and sat back, silent in his thoughts.

"Different how, Mr. Brighton?" Manning said.

"Call me Frank."

"OK — different how, Frank?"

"Blake always had a thing for girls... But they never stuck around very long."

"So, she never made any lasting connections?" Manning said.

"Not really. I think she thought she had to take care of me. Or figured I wouldn't approve. Who the hell knows."

"How long ago did Blake leave?"

Frank Brighton glanced at his watch. "Couple hours I guess."

"She say where she was going?" Colefield asked.

"Nope?"

"Any guesses?"

"Idaho maybe."

"She have friends there?" Manning asked.

"She did. But they moved to Arizona. She likes camping there though."

Frank Brighton downed his drink and got up. "I'm getting another, sure you deputies don't want anything?"

Colefield badly wanted a beer but passed. Manning said she'd take a glass of water. When he returned, he had poured himself another drink and had a bottle of water, which he handed to Manning, before he sat back down.

"My little girl isn't a bad person."

"What has she done, Frank?" Colefield asked.

"I never put two and two together," he said. "Until one night I walked in on her. Caught her naked in bed with a neighbor girl. I did my best raising her after my wife died. Thought we got along fine. It came as kind of a shock to find out she was a lesbian."

"Don't take this wrong," Manning said. "But you don't seem like the liberal type. She must have thought you would be angry."

"I got over it. That's not the main thing I need to tell you ... you know what those little sissy pricks did to her in high school? They raped her. I wanted to bust their heads in, but she wouldn't tell me who was responsible. She told me to forget about it. She came home all bruised up. I could tell something bad happened. She finally broke down and told me."

"And you didn't call the principal or the police?"

"She told me not to. She said it happened because they knew she was a lesbian. Dumb bastards thought they could turn her around..."

Colefield felt things were about to get uglier. *Just how many whiskeys had he had?*

"I suppose I don't need to tell you that this strike has everyone at each other's throats."

"It sure does but can we stay on track," Colefield said and rubbed the scar on his cheek, wondering where the conversation was going next.

"She did it all for me..."

"What are you talking about?" Colefield asked. "Did what?"

"She was hurt. She trusted the PI with her affections..."

"You mean, Ms. Kerns?"

"She seduced my little girl to get information about the union. And she got what she wanted. Then Kerns passed off the information to the Port. After they had enough proof, they called my union boss and put their foot down. Said they had dirt on some of us and if we didn't end this strike soon, heads would roll ... and I would lose everything."

Colefield was starting to put it together. "That's why Blake stole her computer and eventually set fire to her storage locker...?"

"The bitch had copies of everything. Blake didn't know that. She didn't want me to lose my job because of her mistake. She was trying to help."

"If what you said is true, a judge will see that. Did Blake push her off the balcony?"

"She said it was an accident and I believe her. My daughter doesn't lie..."

"What about the ship's captain? Did she mention him?"

"No..."

"He died from a head wound. Did you know that Blake wore an ankle baton when she jogged?"

"My little girl wouldn't kill anybody."

"Did you know about the baton?"

"Who do you think showed her how to use it effectively. She said she was afraid of the homeless and she wanted protection. She was going to buy pepper spray, but I told her to get one of those telescoping batons instead. Cops use them all the time. They're much more effective during a confrontation."

"We need to find her, Frank," Manning said. "You got to help us put an end to this. There's still time to do the right thing."

Frank Brighton's head fell back against the cushion. He threw his drink back and missed the end table when he went to place his empty glass down, instead banging the table leg loudly, startling the deputies.

"Frank," Manning said. "Where is she?"

He started to stand up and then fell backward into the chair. His head hit the cushion and he closed his eyes.

Manning started toward him.

About then, he came around, lifted his head slightly, pointing toward the window.

Colefield turned. There was nothing outside but harsh sunlight and an expansive view of the Columbia River.

"One more time, where is she?"

Brighton started to speak but couldn't find the words. He closed his eyes like he was finally down for the count...

"Let him sleep it off," Colefield said, and pulled out his notebook. "Call Feinstein. Tell him to put out an APB on his daughter suspected of driving a 2013 Thor Outlaw Motor Coach, plate number AGH 711."

31

The following day they still had no word on Blake
Brighton's whereabouts. The alert had gone out for the
Thor Outlaw Motor Coach. Colefield figured she could be
anywhere. Likely, holed up in the woods, just waiting until
things cooled off. She was smart enough to know to stay
out of sight and bright enough to know not to leave any
evidence behind. A shakedown of her room had turned up
nothing.

Colefield went into the office. Deputy Weaver was
sitting at his desk, listening to the marine radio. Chatter
was active on the water.

"Where is everyone?"

"Bart and Manning took the sled. They didn't think
you were coming in. Isn't this your day off?"

Weaver was a big hairy guy with a big heart. A family
man with two kids, a boy and a girl.

"You seem on edge."

Colefield took a deep breath and let it out slowly.
Weaver was probably right.

"Manning say anything to you this morning?"
Colefield said.

"Just that she was heading out on patrol with Bart."

"Nothing on Blake Brighton?"

He shook his head. "Oh, she did say that Feinstein
sent a cruiser over to the Brighton's residence to pick up
the father for more questioning."

"Feinstein call here?"

"Nope."

Colefield sat down at his desk and fired up his computer. After a few minutes, Weaver went back to work. Every time a noise sounded outside, Colefield caught himself looking toward the door.

He printed out his report, tossed it on the Lieutenant's desk, grabbed his cap and headed out the door.

The sun was warm on his weary eyes. He breathed in the outdoors, watched a few of the boaters backing down the boat ramp and started to leave when his cell rang.

He pulled it out and checked the caller ID. It was Jill. He couldn't face her right now, so he let it ring, and ring, before changing his mind and picking up.

Her voice sounded a million miles away...

* * *

Back at his houseboat, he was still playing their conversation over in his head. He needed a distraction and rest. So he decided to grab several cold Heinekens from the fridge and head over toward Montgomery's deck with his fishing rod. Along the way, he bumped into Dr. Irish, standing at Montgomery's front door.

"Hey Doc..." he said, surprised.

"Hi Jason. You live here?"

"In the tender behind you. Montgomery is my slumlord."

"How charming. Do you know if he's home?"

"He rarely goes out. Is something wrong with him?"

"No, no. It's just a routine visit. I want to see how his new pacemaker is working out. But, afterwards, if you've got a minute, I'd like to talk to you about Elizabeth..."

"Sure."

Nearly a half-hour passed before Dr. Becky Irish walked out onto the deck where Colefield was sitting in a ratty lawn chair, fishing. He'd just finished his second beer and looked moderately content.

"That landlord of yours is quite a guy," Becky said, and flopped down in a newer lawn chair that Colefield had put out for her. "He said he ran his own advertising agency here on the houseboat. That true?"

"It is."

"And he wrestled alligators?"

"He did."

"I've never met anyone quite like him."

"He's definitely one of a kind."

"And I thought Elizabeth was a handful."

"How is she?"

"Better... She also mentioned what she asked you to do. I hate to say it, but that might have been a waste of your time."

"I spoke to all of them. They all have alibis for the days in question. I came up with a big fat zero."

"There's a reason for that. Actually, no one broke in after all. The truth is, she's been having mild seizures. I ran her bloodwork and she came up positive for low blood sugar and then followed up with an MRI. The imagery indicated she has signs of epilepsy, which explains her sudden loss of consciousness and memory loss. I've started her on medication that should control the seizures. We talked about it. She thinks these spells of hers came on shortly after one of her last scuba diving trips. We don't know enough about the science to really know what triggers these events."

"Will it affect her work?"

"No, it shouldn't."

"She's a hell of a judge."

"That she is. I'm just glad we found it before she was seriously injured."

"Well I think that's worth celebrating. Can I get you a beer?"

She stood up. "No, I've got to get back to work. But I'll take a raincheck."

"Of course."

Colefield walked her to her car. She got in and rolled down her window.

"Keep an eye on Montgomery. He thinks he's invincible but he's not..."

32

That night Colefield rolled out of the marina parking lot in his pickup. He headed up Harney Street and turned right at the first intersection. He eventually crossed the Sellwood Bridge and about two blocks from there he noticed a dark sedan following him. The sedan had followed him from the marina. He stayed on Macadam for a few miles, checking his rearview mirror periodically, until he reached John's Landing and turned into the parking lot, killed his lights and waited. The dark sedan made a left at the light and followed him into the parking lot and stopped. Colefield got out and walked up to the driver's door, his hand on his holster. The sedan's tinted window came down.

It was Manning's Ex, wearing the same cheap yellow suit and smirk.

"You should have taken my advice," Manning's Ex said.

Colefield kept his guard up. "Never been know to take advice from scumbags."

"That hurt."

"Continue to follow me, I'll end your career."

"Doubtful, lover-boy."

"Leave her alone," Colefield said.

"She's my wife. You're an adulterer. I think you're shit."

"Fuck you."

"Stay away from her..."

"It's her choice," Colefield said.

"I never filed the subpoena. She's still legally married."

"And you're full of shit and an embarrassment to the force," Colefield said.

The window rolled up and the sedan drove off. Colefield watched it drive out of the lot and head down a side street. Suddenly, he felt very weary walking back to his pickup.

Colefield drove north, keeping an eye on his mirrors but he didn't see any signs of the sedan.

He thought about the encounter, how it spiked his blood pressure, sent a wave of anxiety through his chest. He tried to blow it off but couldn't. It clung on like a cancerous growth.

*   *   *

Her plane was late by one hour and ten minutes. He'd hung out at the cell phone waiting area until he got bored and then just drove around aimlessly, killing time.

She was flying Delta. She eventually called him at 10:45 from baggage claim and said she had arrived. She'd meet him curbside.

He made two loops before he saw Jill standing outside the terminal with her suitcases, looking rung out. She waved when she saw his pickup approach. He still felt a pang of emotion and tenderness.

She had on a slinky black tank-top, white shorts and leather sandals that showed off her ankle tattoo.

He pulled to the curb, hopped out to give her a hand with her luggage.

They smiled at each other and kissed. It seemed awkward though.

"I'm glad you're back," he said, picking up her luggage.

"You don't know how happy I am to be home. My mother is a royal bitch."

He loaded the suitcases into the back of the pickup and opened the passenger door for her. Then he climbed in behind the wheel and they exited the airport.

She began talking about her trip to NYC and he took in what he could, while driving down Columbia toward Jantzen Beach, where she owned a small condominium.

"Dad and I put mother in rehab before I left."

"Sounds like rehab may be good for her."

"None of it's true...what she said...it was lies."

"You didn't go to your high school reunion?"

"That 's not what I meant."

"Look, I understand. Sometimes we don't make the best choices."

"I never slept with him, Jason. He was a close friend in high school. I stayed with him for three days because he's dying of pancreatic cancer. I'm a fuckin' wreck over it. And all my mother cares about is herself and what she can destroy. How fucked-up is that?"

"Pretty fucked-up."

"You seem different. Are you happy to see me?"

Colefield swallow hard. "Of course, I am."

Jill stared at him. Her eyes were tired but perceptive, but she didn't have the energy to probe, which was just as well.

After they parked, he carried her bags up to her condo front door. She had trouble putting her key into the slot. Nerves.

"I should go, he said."

"I want you to stay. Let me rephrase that. I need you to stay..."

* * *

Sunlight flittered in the through the thin lacy curtains landing on the bed and their naked bodies.

Colefield felt the warm light and sat up. Jill was still asleep, curled up on her side, her back to him. Her skin looked tan and smooth and groomed, her ass picture perfect. Everything about her was about style and grace. Compared to Manning, she was a domestic cat. Manning was wild and dangerous. Manning's muscular body was ripped, her skin rough, her hands strong. They looked like they could claw your eyes out. Jill's hands were working hands, too, but different, smaller and flawless.

Colefield laid there for a while longer staring at her. He had to go, he was running late. Yet, he held on to the moment, as if it was going to be their last intimate contact.

He eventually gathered his things and left quietly.

When he reached the curb, he looked back at the condo. He felt hollow and lost and thought about all the times he had been with Jill and remembered the best and the worse and walked away knowing it was time, but not knowing if it was right. He still loved her but was it enough?

Manning saw the change in him when he got to work. She was alone in the front office. The Lieutenant's office door was ajar, and he could hear him talking on the telephone.

"She's back, isn't she?" Manning said, staring.

"Yep."

"Did you tell her?"

"No."

"Are you going to?"

"I don't know..."

She swallowed hard. "So, are we done now?"

"No."

"Then when are you going to tell her?"

"She's had a rough trip. I'll tell her when it's time."

She lowered her voice. "I think I love you, Jason. I want you to know that."

"I think I love you, too."

They made plans to have pizza and catch a flick at the Hollywood Theatre after work. They could talk then. Discuss their future.

Lieutenant hung up the telephone and called Colefield into his office.

Colefield poked his head in the door. "You want to see me?"

"Close the door," the Lieutenant said. "And take a seat."

Colefield glanced back at Manning, shut the door and took a seat.

The Lieutenant looked up from a stack of paperwork. "Manning working out?" The lieutenant said, looking him in the eye.

He nearly coughed before he found the right words. "In my opinion, she's an asset to the team."

"At least, I hear she is to you," the Lieutenant said.

"Sir?"

"Ah, damn, Jason you know what the hell I'm talking about."

Colefield paused. "I do, sir. I won't let it affect our working relationship."

"Well, don't let this turn into a soap opera."

"Yes, sir."

"How's the Kerns case going?"

"We still haven't located Blake Brighton."

"Find her and close the damn case."

33

Colefield showered and changed out of his uniform at work, then drove to Manning's apartment in SE. She was drying her hair when he arrived.

"Just give me five minutes," she said, and walked back into the bathroom. Through the open door, he could see her image in the large mirror. She cleaned up nice. She had put on some makeup and a short red dress, heels, and some beaded jewelry. She finished blow drying her hair, smiling at him. Colefield sat down on the sofa and felt uneasy.

"Help yourself to a beer in the fridge," she said.

"I'll pass."

"Then grab me one, would you?"

Colefield stood up. "Where's Roxy?"

"She's with my neighbor across the street. Richard drove by my place twice last night and I don't feel comfortable leaving her home alone."

Just the thought of her ex keeping an eye on her made his blood boil.

When he got to the refrigerator, he had changed his mind about the beer and pulled out two, popped the caps, and carried them into the bathroom. Manning set her hair dryer down on the counter and took one of the beers.

"Cheers!" she said.

They clinked bottles and drank.

"Richard and I had an encounter," Colefield said. "He threatened me. Now he's driving by your place. He's got to be stopped."

"He came to your houseboat?"

"Parking lot. When I left, he followed me for a few miles until I pulled over and confronted him."

He filled her in...

"The bastard is a real pain in the ass," she said.

"He'll move on..."

"You don't know Richard. He's persistent. He usually gets what he wants in the end. Right now, it's to make my life a living hell ... If it wasn't for you, I'd probably move to Idaho to get away from him."

"Don't let that asshole win. You're tougher than that."

"You're right." She set her beer down and kissed him on the lips.

They finished their beers and left. They took his truck and drove to the Hollywood District, had a slice of pizza down the street from the Hollywood theatre. The movie started at 8 PM. They arrived early and had good seats near the back. The theatre wasn't crowded. The movie about to play was an action film staring Matt Damon. They watched film clips for upcoming releases and chatted about what they thought would be a good film to see next.

Colefield put his arm around her. She turned and looked at him with warm eyes.

"Want a pizza kiss?" she whispered.

"Sure..."

They kissed. She rested her hand on his thigh, walked it up to his crotch and left it there. He could feel himself growing hard inside his jeans. She rubbed it a few times and then moved her hand away and focused on the big screen.

He put his hand on her leg and slid it up under her dress. She had a concealed weapon strapped to her upper thigh. He moved around it and went up higher. She wasn't wearing panties. He felt her warm moistness, brushed over her pubic hair. She reached over and removed his hand and set it down on her knee. "You get me so hot," she whispered. "Save that thought."

They enjoyed the movie. It was a perfect distraction from work and all the other bullshit. They shared some popcorn and a soft drink.

When the movie ended, they watched the credits run as if neither of them wanted to leave. They were one of the last to exit their seats. In the lobby, Manning told him she needed to use the restroom.

"I'll meet you out front.

Colefield walked out the main door and stood on the sidewalk under the large theatre marque. The bright lights of the sign reminded him of being in Las Vegas. There were people walking about. The air had turned cooler. Most of small shops across the street had closed for the evening. Colefield felt something he couldn't explain. A premonition of sorts. He scanned the sidewalks and the rooftop parking structure across the street. Some cars left, but he still felt someone was watching him. He kept looking but didn't see anything out of the ordinary.

Manning walked out the front door. He started to walk toward her when the gunshots rang out.

34

Everyone around them made a run for it. Manning was hit. Colefield grabbed onto her as she went limp in his arms. He eased her down on the sidewalk. She had been shot twice in the chest, two center of mass shots. The third round was meant for her head, but it only grazed her scalp.

He looked across the street and saw the shooter on the rooftop flee.

Manning was gasping for air, blood spilling from her wounds. Her eyes pleaded up at him. One of her lungs had been punctured. The sucking chest wound sounded fatal. He applied pressure to her wounds, but it was hopeless, blood was everywhere, oozing down over her dress and onto the sidewalk. The haunted look on her face was one he'd never forget...

"Hang on," Colefield told her, pulling out his cell, blood covering his hands. He called it in. Help was coming...

She was trying to hang on. She squeezed his hand weakly. She attempted to lift her head but couldn't. He leaned in, turned his ear to her lips. She was trying to say something, but her words were mostly garbled. Yet, she wouldn't give up, hung on for a few moments more, until she got out: "I love you..."

Hang on...please...

She breathed her final breath. Her head rolled to the side. She was gone.

Colefield felt his world crash down around him. This could not be happening.

She couldn't be dead...

A wave of anger exploded inside him, rocketing him back to his senses. He pulled out his concealed .38 Police Special, kept crouched down, scanned the rooftop parking lot across the street where the shots had come from, where he saw the shooter flee. He caught a glimpse of a masked man running across the lot. Sirens were approaching now, yet they brought him no comfort. It was too late for her. He took off running toward the parking structure in a flurry of anger and rage.

There was only one exit from the rooftop. It was at the back of the building. Just ahead of him, a few cars spilt out onto the street, a red Taurus, a Blue Chevy Van. They were not the shooter's vehicles, because he made out a dark sedan that he believed was.

He threw every muscle and ounce of energy toward reaching the exit before it was too late: before the car came barreling down the ramp, before he could stop it.

The last time he had put so much effort into running, he was back in the game, charging toward the goal line, sweating, determined, the glare of stadium lights shining down on him, the turf hard as pavement, the crowd shouting.

He rounded the last corner of the building, breathless, waiting with gun drawn by the narrow exit. He was looking up at a cave barely wide enough for a vehicle to pass through. There should be headlights by now. What was wrong?

Where was the bastard?

If he wasn't coming down, then Colefield was going up. He sprinted up the dark ramp, ready for anything.

He heard an engine idling somewhere. He stepped out onto the rooftop. Keeping low, staying in the shadows, he saw the sedan just sitting there, like a bull ready to charge. Then the driver gunned it, heading toward him, high-beams glaring.

Colefield got off one shot before he lunged out of the car's path. The bullet hit a front tire and sent the car straight into the side of the ramp wall. Metal scraped against the concrete, sparks flew, but the vehicle was still moving. Colefield rolled up on his heels and got off two more shots. People on the street screamed. And then he heard glass shatter somewhere nearby. He ran back down the ramp and saw the sedan had crashed through a shop window before coming to a stop inside, the horn stuck on, blaring. Dust and smoke began to funnel out as Colefield approached.

Steam from a busted radiator smoldered out from under the crumpled hood. White powder hung in the air of the interior from the deployed airbags and he struggled to see through the rear window. After the eerie dust finally settled, he saw the bloody head — a portion of it missing. Bits of brain matter leaked out of the fresh wound. It had been a hell of shot. Colefield's bullets had penetrated the rear window and one found its target — through the back of his skull. It exited out his right orbital lobe, leaving behind a gaping hole.

Richard Manning had finally met his match...

Colefield found a hunk of metal and pried open the driver's door. He checked the neck for a pulse. There was none.

He began a search of the interior. He found a Glock inside a holster clipped to the belt but no rifle.

He popped the trunk lid and looked inside. The rifle case had slid forward almost out of sight. Inside it was an AR-15 with a laser scope, modified stock and set to fire on semi-auto. Four magazines holding 30 rounds each were also there. The magazine in the rifle was missing three rounds.

It made him feel sick.

He slammed the trunk closed and walked away from the settling debris. Out on the sidewalk, two uniformed officers stepped into the light and drew down on him.

Colefield knew the drill and put his hands up.

35

Internal affairs grilled him for hours and then released him. The lieutenant placed him on paid administrative leave while the case got sorted out. He could barely keep his mind on his driving crossing the Sellwood Bridge. The orange sunrise was almost too bright on his bloodshot eyes. He crossed the yellow line and heard a horn blast and yanked the wheel to get his pickup back in his lane. It was then that he remembered Roxy and made a U-turn and headed toward Manning's apartment.

He parked across the street and began knocking on doors until he found the right house — the neighbor who was babysitting the dog. She was a single mother with two teenagers and was running late, she said to him on the front porch. He introduced himself and she invited him inside.

"Do you smell that?"

She ran back into the kitchen. He could smell toast burning, heard some cupboards slam close. He walked into the kitchen.

"I've got some bad news..." he said, feeling the rush of pain funneling back into him.

She turned and frowned. "Please don't tell me it's Bev..."

He told her everything. Gave her time to absorb it. She flopped down at the kitchen table, put her head in her hands and broke down. He listened to her sobs and it sounded like his own soul echoing grief.

She snapped out of it, grabbed a Kleenex and blew her noise. "What shall we do about Roxy?"

"I was kind-of-hoping you could keep her."

"I can't. We can't. Our landlord won't allow it. She's going to have to go to a shelter, I'm sorry."

The teenagers came out together, rubbing sleepy eyes, still in pajamas. Roxy came running out behind them. When she saw Colefield standing there, tired, weary expression, the dog sensed something was wrong, and knelt at his feet.

She knew...

"I can't take her to a shelter. I'll find a home for her," Colefield said.

"Mom? What's going on?"

"He's a police officer. I'll tell you later. Go to your rooms and get dressed."

"Where's Auntie?"

That was the name they had for Manning.

"Go to your rooms. Please!"

She walked over to a hall closet and pulled out a leash. She handed it to Colefield.

"What's going to happen to her things?"

"Does she have any relatives in the area?"

"I don't think so."

"Then it'll be up to her landlord. Someone will be in touch with him."

"Thanks for doing this. I would keep Roxy if I could."

Colefield clipped the leash to Roxy's collar and started toward the door.

"She mentioned you. She said you were a decent man..."

*   *   *

That week, Calico Jack wasn't sure how he liked sharing the houseboat with a dog. He kept his distance, spending most of his time outside or on the windowsill. Colefield had to put Roxy in a different room when it was time to feed the cat. Roxy was having issues. She was restless and out-of-sorts, kept going to the sliding glass door and looking out, as if she thought Manning was going to show up any moment. Colefield knew he couldn't keep her, but he hadn't been able to find someone that would. Montgomery put down the law. The dog couldn't stay past the end of the month or else...

Then, on a Tuesday, Bart showed up at his door. Colefield's first impulse was to convince Bart to take her.

"Hi Colefield. How you been?"

Colefield looked like shit. Stubble on his chin. Greasy shorts. Faded t-shirt. Hair uncombed.

"Crappy. How are you?"

Bart glanced around. Colefield's living conditions were a train wreck. There were empties lying everywhere, clothing slung over the backs of chairs, dirty socks left out, dishes stacked in the sink, a carton of milk on the counter, garbage sacks stacked up by the door, stinking up the place.

"Everyone wonders when you're coming back."

"When I'm ready."

"That's what the Lieutenant said."

"How 'bout taking a German Shephard off my hands?"

Roxy wandered over and sniffed Bart's shoes. Flies buzzed Colefield who in the worst way needed a shower.

"Sorry, I got a dog."

"Manning trained her. She'd be a good dog for you."

"Can't do it..."

"So, you just happen to be in the neighborhood, thought you'd pay my pathetic ass a visit?"

"Vancouver State Troopers found the Thor Motor Coach. Thought you might be interested..."

Colefield looked very much interested. "It's about damn time. You want a beer?"

Bart frowned. "No, I want you to get dressed and come with me to look at the wreckage."

"They arrest Blake Brighton?"

"No."

"Why not?"

"You'll see. Come with me..."

Colefield looked at his piles of clutter, took a whiff of his underarms. He smelled worse than roadkill.

"I need a shower first."

They drove for nearly an hour, crossing the I-205 Bridge and then heading east on Highway 14. The highway ran through the Gorge, winding its way through the fertile countryside and then miles of dense trees. They eventually passed a RV park and then a few miles later, a well-known hiking area — Beacon Rock, a monolith of granite protruding out over the cliff's edge.

After another long section of narrow highway, with more tight turns, the road began to climb.

At mile post 29 they slowed. A few hundred feet ahead Colefield saw the flashing lights. State Police had blocked off a section of road and had traffic down to one lane. Bart pulled onto the tight shoulder and parked.

They spoke with the cop in charge and he pointed toward a section of missing guardrail.

"She went off the road there," the officer said. "A boater discovered the body this morning and called us."

"Any witnesses?"

"Just one. The paramedics are treating her. She claims she jumped from the vehicle before it crashed through the guardrail. We picked her up about a mile down the road. She said she was going for help."

"Who is she?"

"Hitchhiker. Young girl. At the wrong place at the wrong time."

"Is there a way we can get down to see the scene?" Colefield asked.

"If you walk about three-hundred feet back down the highway, you'll see a small clearing with a steep trail down to the river. Take it easy though. One of our officers almost broke his neck trying to get down to it."

Colefield looked over at Bart. "Let's go talk to the girl first."

They walked over to the paramedic's truck. The back doors were open. A teenager with purple hair and dirty jeans, sat on the bumper while a paramedic bandaged a small flesh wound on her forehead. A filthy backpack sat on the ground. The girl had ebony eyes, pouty lips and facial piercings. Her palms and arms looked liked they gone through a thicket of briar. A faded jean jacket rested over one knee. She had on a worn t-shirt with the lettering "Stinky Pinky" on the front.

She looked over at the deputies.

"I understand you witnessed the accident last night." Colefield said to her.

"Duh. Crazy bitch was out of her mind."

"What's your name?"

"Can't you read?" She pointed to her t-shirt.

Colefield smirked. "I doubt that's your name."

Bart turned toward the paramedic. "Is she going to be all right?"

"Good as new after I finish up here." The paramedic said. "Her name's Cher. At least that's what she told me."

The girl pouted at the paramedic.

"Got a last name, Cher?" Colefield said.

"Nope."

"You a runaway?" Bart said.

"I can take care of myself."

"What is your connection to Ms. Brighton?"

"The dead bitch? She got what was coming to her."

"That's not what I asked you."

"Bitch offered me a ride. I took it. Then she tries to glide on me. I wasn't havin' it."

"She made a pass at you?" Colefield said.

"Duh. I told her if she tried it again, I'd break her arm."

"Did she?"

"She tried, but I stopped her."

"Then what happened?"

She slowed down for the corner. I figured it was my last chance to be done with the whore. So I bailed out the passenger door."

"That how you got all bruised up?" Bart said.

"Did you really ask me that?"

"OK — Cher." Colefield said. "Maybe we got off to a rocky start. We just want to know what happened. We're not trying to jerk your shit."

She almost smiled.

Colefield gave her a moment. "What happened next?"

"I guess the bitch freaked, because she didn't make the corner, just drove straight into the guardrail and poof, the RV was gone."

"You saw it happen?"

"Duh..."

"I thought you said you jumped out while it was moving. You must have hit the ground pretty hard."

"Yeah..."

"Did she apply brakes?"

"All I heard was metal, man. After that, it sounded like the earth was shaking apart."

36

After the deputies got her full statement, they looked for the clearing the officer had mentioned. Bart was the one to spot the trail. It was steep, narrow, but doable. Bart said he'd go first.

"We have some rope in the cruiser?"

"Yeah — let me get it before you try this."

Bart tossed Colefield the keys and waited by the side of the road. After a few minutes, Colefield returned carrying a coil of rope.

He handed one end to Bart. "Tie that around you."

Colefield walked over to the nearest tree and looped the rope around it. Bart figured out what to do next.

"Once you get down to that big rock stop. That should be about the end of the rope. I'll come down and then we'll tie the end around the boulder."

"Got it."

Bart went first. He made it around the worst section of stumps and rocks with only a few minor stumbles. Colefield went next. They both reached the rock and tied off and did the same thing again until they worked themselves down to flat ground.

Colefield saw the wreckage beyond a strand of trees, partially in the water. They hiked over to it. There were two paramedics in climbing harnesses that were searching the area around the crash site.

Both sides of the Motor Coach were caved in. The windshield was busted out. Tires blown. It looked as if the vehicle had come to a stop after rolling over many times.

Colefield studied the path that he figured the Coach had made. He counted two broken trees snapped off at their bases, which is where he figured the bus started losing speed. It then rolled across the rocky riverbank. He could see broken glass and traces of yellow paint everywhere. The vehicle had nearly plunged into the river before it wedged up against two boulders.

What remained of her body had been placed into a body bag. It had been carried away from the water and temporarily placed in a clearing. Colefield walked over and unzipped the bag. She was pretty busted up, almost unrecognizable.

One of the paramedics walked over.

"You know her?"

"Yep."

"Not very pretty."

"Where'd you find her?"

"She was thrown from the vehicle," he said, and then pointed behind him toward the riverbank. "We found her lying over there. Her head was submerged in a couple feet of river water."

"She have a baton strapped to her leg?"

"No, sir."

Colefield walked over to where the man had pointed. He saw some fresh blood on a couple rocks and more floating in a puddle.

He searched the area, back tracked toward the RV, and eventually found what he was looking for in the shadows. It had almost gone undetected. There on the ground was the baton.

He shouted back to the paramedic. "You have any plastic bags on you?"

"Sure!"

"I need one."

The paramedic pulled one from a medical kit and carried it over.

"How do you plan on transporting the body?"

"The National Guard offered. One of their helicopters is coming for her."

"What's that on the ground?"

"Something that will hopefully close this case."

37

The robust hike back up the steep hillside left Colefield tired but somehow recharged spiritually. Maybe it was the smell of the woods or the crisp open air or just pushing his body beyond what he thought he could do. But something had cracked loose and he felt better.

Bart noticed the change. Colefield seemed a little more cheerful when they reached the top and stopped to catch their breath.

"That was kind of a bitch," Bart said, looking back down over the edge of the cliff.

"Maybe we can skip the Fitness Test this year ... think the Lieutenant would go for it?"

Bart grinned.

The deputies walked up toward the State Troopers. Colefield asked around until he found the right cop who had been down to search the wreckage earlier.

He was a stout-looking man, probably five years on the job. Colefield briefed him on the Kerns case.

"I read about the girl in the fountain. You took lead on it?"

"I had a partner who helped."

"We heard about her. Damn loss. Sorry, deputy."

"Have you talked with Cher over there?"

The officer adjusted his cap. "We think she stole ID from a motorist at the country store off Highway 14. You guys probably passed it on your way. We sent an officer there and he spoke with the owner of the store. The owner said he remembered the Motor Coach pulling in for fuel.

The young girl was hitchhiking, and he thinks she got in with the girl driving the RV after pickpocketing one of the customers."

Colefield started to walk away with Bart and then stopped, looked back at the officer.

"Next of kin been notified?"

"Couldn't reach 'em."

"I might be able to help with that."

38

On Friday, three weeks after Manning's death, Colefield went back to work. He wasn't sure how he was going to react when he entered the office. He had Roxy with him. The dog immediately tugged hard on her leash and headed straight for Manning's empty chair. Colefield unclipped her and Roxy jumped up on it and sprawled out, took ownership.

There was no one else in the office but the two of them, which was what he had hoped, because he felt like shit inside. It was a hollow emptiness that was damn near suffocating. And he knew he had to do something to escape its hold over him.

The marine radio squawked, so he started toward it and picked up the mic. He gave his call sign, but no one answered. Strange. So he hung up the mic and glanced out the window.

There was the familiar trail of boaters offloading or loading watercraft at the boat ramp and bikini clad woman baking their bodies along the beach. The activity blended together, and he couldn't seem to concentrate on any of it — a movie screen out of focus.

He looked back at Roxy and thought he smelled CRP oil coming from Manning's desk. It brought back the memory of the day he came in while she was cleaning her weapon. Her dark eyes were so focused. She was competent, skilled, a real pro. He knew he had to do something fast to take his mind off her and walked into the small kitchen and filled a bowl with water, carried it back out and placed it down on the floor within sight of Roxy, who was not budging from the chair.

He stared at the dog. "There's water... Aren't you thirsty?"

Roxy ignored him, remained planted in the seat. Her head on her paws.

He didn't blame her.

He realized it was still to soon for either of them.

He made up every excuse possible to try and leave, but her spirit was in the room, keeping him there, whispering that it was going to be OK. He could do this.

Get to work ... get on with it ...

About then, Bart and Weaver walked in the office door. Roxy sat up and began barking.

The two deputies froze and looked at Colefield.

He looked over at Roxy. "It's OK girl."

His words calmed her, and she laid back down on the chair.

The deputies were apprehensive.

After a long moment he said: "Aren't you going to say something?"

Bart and Weaver looked at each other.

Bart broke the silence. "Welcome back."

39

On Sunday, Colefield carried Roxy's 25-pound bag of dry food and her bowls up to his pickup and threw them in back. He went back to his houseboat and called the dog over and fastened her leash. He led her up the boat ramp and let do her business in the fresh cut grass before putting her in the cab of the truck.

The drive went smoothly. Roxy seemed more relaxed suddenly. Even when they pulled into Big Eddy's Marina and parked, she didn't bark.

Colefield partially rolled down the passenger and driver side windows and left Roxy in the cab. She watched him walk down the ramp leading to Judge Brown's houseboat.

There was no drone buzzing overhead this time. Big Eddy was either gone or not flying today. He walked over to Judge Brown's door and knocked.

He could hear footsteps approaching from inside. The door opened. Judge Brown had her coat on and was holding her purse.

"Deputy Colefield, how are you?"

"Fine Elizabeth. I was going to ask you the same..."

"Couldn't be better. I'm afraid you caught me at a bad time. I was just leaving to meet Becky. You remember my friend, right?"

"Sure. This won't take long. I just wanted to fill you in about your friend Ms. Kris Kerns."

"Oh, dear ... in that case you'd better come inside."

He entered her house and followed the judge into the living room and took a seat. The judge sat opposite him on the sofa.

"I've been meaning to call but every time I go for my phone, I hesitate. I felt I needed to tell you in person."

"I appreciate that. I read about it in the paper that you found the girl responsible. I was also sorry to hear about your partner. She seemed like a nice young woman."

"Well, most of what I'm going to tell you, you might have already read. But I want you to know that your friend was responsible for bringing to light the corruption inside the Longshoreman's union. You probably know that she was investigating several workers in the union who were hell-bent on sabotaging any efforts made by the ICTSI who operated Port Terminals to keep cargo flowing."

"Yes, I am aware of this."

"What you might not know is that her former concierge's father was actually one of the men she was investigating. Blake Brighton believed that Ms. Kerns had used her friendship with her to get dirt on her father. I don't think she did. I believe what really happened was that Brighton had a fatal attraction to your friend and walked in on her having sex with the captain of the *Piranha*. According to a crew member we spoke to, their affair had been going on for several years. She couldn't handle that and became so enraged that she pushed your friend off the balcony. The captain saw it all. But he was concerned he'd be a suspect and kept the truth from us. Before we could get the facts, he was killed by Blake Brighton. I recovered the murder weapon at the RV wreckage and the MA has confirmed it was the weapon used to kill the captain."

"What a disturbed poor girl."

"You had an honorable friend. I felt you needed to hear the facts."

"Thank you, Jason. That means a lot."

Colefield stood up. "Tell Dr. Irish I said hello."

"Of course. If you don't mind, I'm going to sit here for a few minutes and let it all sink in."

Colefield showed himself out and instead of heading back toward his pickup, he turned and walked over to the maintenance man's houseboat and rapped on the door.

Ricky Foster, Fred's nephew, answered the door.

"Deputy Colefield how are you?"

"Fine, Ricky, is your uncle around?"

"Yeah, let me get him."

After a moment, Fred came to the door. "Deputy Colefield what can I do for you?"

Colefield could see Ricky listening in on their conversation inside the room.

"Could I speak to you in private?"

"Sure." Fred stepped outside and closed the door. "What's this about, deputy?"

Colefield leaned in and kept his voice low. He spoke with Fred for a few minutes and then Fred nodded his head.

"Let me get Ricky." Fred said, and opened the door.

"Ricky! C'mon out here."

Ricky appeared looking a little worried that he had done something wrong.

Colefield smiled. "Let's take a walk Ricky."

Ricky looked at his uncle. "Ah, OK..."

Colefield led the way toward his pickup. A few yards away, he turned to Ricky. "Wait here." he said.

Ricky stopped, looking confused.

Colefield walked over to his pickup and got Roxy. He led her around the back of the truck toward Ricky.

The boy's eyes lit up like fireworks. Colefield handed him Roxy's leash. "She's yours if you want her." Colefield said.

"Really! How cool. Yes, of course I want her." The boy spun around and looked at his uncle, who had walked up.

"Is it OK?"

"I may have some explaining to do to your mother, but we'll work something out."

Ricky thanked Colefield several more times before he jogged down the ramp with Roxy trotting along beside him.

Fred approached the deputy and shook his hand. "That was a fine thing you did for Ricky. Maybe it'll make all the difference in him now."

"I think my former partner would be happy. I've got some dry food and bowls in the truck."

Fred tossed the bag over his shoulder and collected the bowls. "Thanks again, deputy. Come and visit anytime."

"I might just do that."

Colefield climbed back in his truck and watched Fred walk down to the marina.

This time karma worked out...

Smiling, he started his truck wiping a tear away as he headed home.

—THE END—

ACKNOWLEDGMENTS

Writing takes a team effort, and I have one of the very best. I owe many thanks to my devoted group of first readers who have over the years stuck with me without complaint to the very bitter end. I may have plied them with liquor and gifts to keep them going but it was worth it. Many of their views were taken to heart and implemented in this book. I'd like to give them a big applause: Matthew Beck; Bennett McGough; Harley L. Sachs; and a very special thanks to writer Bill Johnson. I was honored to have his help again on this project.

I'd also like to thank all of the independent bookstores and libraries, especially Multnomah County Library, that stock my previous books (and that I hope will add this book to their shelves) and for inviting me to do readings and signings.

I also owe another thumbs up to Multnomah County River Patrol. *River City* and *River Rat* wouldn't have happened without their and Deputy Jason Tyrus' willingness to show me the ropes of what life is like on the River Patrol. They kindly took me out on the water for the real deal adventure as they policed Portland's "Liquid Highways". Hopefully once again my broad descriptions of the River Patrol Headquarters, its procedures, and of the team of dedicated officers who keep the waterways a safer place will meet with their approval.

Finally, thank you to my beautiful and talented Birdie, my fearless partner in crime. Her re-writing efforts ignited my manuscript and shot this novel to life. Without her, I would just be another lonely River Rat, a

Whaler of Words. She's the best first mate a captain could ever ask for....

River Blues was written aboard the *Enterprise* in Portland, Oregon.

ABOUT THE AUTHOR

Doc Macomber is a native Northwesterner. His previous books include: *The Killer Coin, Wolf's Remedy, Snip, Riff Raff* – a finalist in the Killer Nashville Claymore Award, *River City*, a Silver Medal Winner in the 2015 Benjamin Franklin Awards from the Independent Book Publishers Association in the Mystery/Suspense category, and *River Rat*. Doc served twenty years in the USAF and USANG and formerly served in a Special Ops unit in Portland, Oregon. He currently lives aboard a trawler in the Pacific Northwest. As a decorated Marine Captain once noted, "Doc sees much ... says little ... and writes it all down."

(Author photograph by Ty Hitzemann)

**Discover Other Titles by Doc Macomber at
Amazon.com:**

(The Jack Vu Mysteries)

The Killer Coin

Wolf's Remedy

Snip

Riff Raff

(The Jason Colefield Mysteries)

River City

River Rat

River Blues

**(Visit your favorite online retailers to purchase
paperback versions, audiobooks, or MP3s.)**

Connect With The Author Online:

I appreciate you reading my book! Please consider writing a review at your favorite online retailer.

Thanks again.

Here are my social media coordinates:

Amazon author page: https://www.amazon.com/Doc-Macomber/e/B001JRZZ8K

Smashwords: http://www.smashwords.com/books/-search?query=Doc+Macomber

LinkedIn: http://www.linkedin.com/pub/doc-macomber/30/681/b58

Website: http://www.docmacomber.com

www.ingramcontent.com/pod-product-compliance
Lightning Source LLC
Chambersburg PA
CBHW031234260626
47169CB00007B/2288